A Merry Little
~Hat Trick~
Christmas

Samantha Wayland

Also by Samantha Wayland

Destiny Calls

With Grace

Hat Trick Book One: Fair Play

Hat Trick Book Two: Two Man Advantage

Hat Trick Book Three: End Game

Crashing the Net

Home & Away

Out of Her League

Checking It Twice

Take the Shot (in the *Changing on the Fly* anthology)

A Merry Little (Hat Trick) Christmas

Published by Loch Awe Press
P.O. Box 5481
Wayland, MA 01778

ISBN 978-1-940839-15-8

Edited by Meghan Miller
       & Chelsea Kuhel (www.madisonseidler.com)
Cover Art by Caitlin Fry

Dedication

For Mr. Wayland and the bug, for being the reason I love Christmas again.

Acknowledgements

Many thanks to my long-time editor, Meghan Miller, without whom I would be lost. Thanks also to Caitlin Fry, who creates my covers beautiful and puts up with my sometimes random and often vague feedback and still manages to make sense of it. And a big thanks to Chelsea Kuhel, who generously took this project on at the last minute.

As always, Stephanie Kay gets the award for the world's most patient cheerleader and whip-cracker (depending on the day). And Victoria Morgan get the award for ruthlessly seeking out and destroying passive voice and excessive adverbs better than anyone. My stories are always, *always* better because of her hard work. She is also responsible for the idea for the candy cane striped...er...gift within this story, though certainly not on purpose.

Chapter One

Henri Girard wasn't born yesterday. God knew, the multiple massive ice packs wrapped around both his knees were testament to that. He picked at the Ace bandages holding them in place and told himself to be patient. He'd played sixteen minutes in tonight's game, and his body wasn't soon going to let him forget it. Too bad the next game was the day after tomorrow, and there were another fifty-something to go in the regular season.

And they were going to make the playoffs, too, if he had anything to say about it.

So went the life, and pains, of a veteran hockey player. He still enjoyed the game, the competition, and the team, even if it hurt a little more every year. It didn't help that the rest of the guys on the team all looked like babies. Good god, they had these fresh faces, almost no scars, and *visors* on their helmets so they had a shot at making it to thirty-six without a face like Henri's.

The sport had changed in a lot of ways since Henri had been drafted at eighteen. In the almost twenty years he'd spent in this league, he'd seen countless players come and go. Teams changed, coaches were fired, management was overhauled, rules improved. He got punched in the head a lot less now, which was nice. And the crackdown on dirty hits meant he might actually have a few years left in him.

He'd been here in Boston for the better part of the last decade, and hoped to finish his career here and retire to the city. His family back in Montreal would be appalled, but he had four kids entrenched in their schools and activities in the community. He had no desire to uproot them. He knew plenty of guys who had been forced to drag their families back-and-forth across the continent because of trades—or worse, guys who'd had to leave their families behind at home so that they could have stability, even if it meant they couldn't see their father much.

That would suck. Henri wasn't about to volunteer this information to management or his agent, but at this point, he'd retire before he moved to a new team. And his hope, which he *was* speaking to management about, was that he'd be able to get a job with the team going forward. Player development sounded pretty good to him. He already spent plenty of time with some of the younger guys, trying to help them keep their heads on straight while millions of dollars, scores of beautiful people, and countless other temptations were within easy grasp.

He could hear two of his less successful projects arguing out in the hallway right now. Well, no—it wasn't fair to call them projects, when in fact Jean-Michel and Noel were his friends. Also, it wasn't fair to call the incessant bickering they were always engaged in "arguing", since that made it sound far more productive, purposeful, and adult than it really was.

Fortunately for the two of them, Henri was one of the only people who understood what they were yelling, as it was all in French. Every once in a while, one of them would say something that would make the team's Athletic Trainer, Savannah Morrison, smile, so Henri suspected she understood the swears, at least, which probably meant she'd learned her share of Quebecoise French in the locker room. If she knew more than that, she'd never let on.

But then, she was pretty good at keeping secrets, Henri suspected.

He watched as she moved efficiently through her space, grabbing what she needed before tackling the next problem. There were always a lot of little things to deal with after a game, and tonight's had been chippy as hell, so a steady stream of guys had come through while Henri had been sitting there. It had taken the team a while to trust her, as not one of them had ever had a female trainer before, but she'd more than proven herself. New guys sometimes paused, but the rest of the team and management made it clear that any shit would not be tolerated.

Hell, no one even made fun of her adorable fuzzy Santa hat, the pompom swaying whenever she bent over her work, and hockey players *never* showed that much restraint when the opportunity to chirp someone arose.

No one would ever admit it—because if they did, Savannah would have their hides—but most of the guys felt a least a little protective of her. Rhian, though, took it to another level. Even now, he sat on one of her tables, his back to the wall and arms crossed over his impressively wide chest, watching her and her staff work. As far as Henri could tell, Rhian didn't have any reason to be there. He must have changed out of his hockey gear and into his game-day suit in record time. His hair was wet, so he'd at least bothered to shower, but he'd shown up not long after Henri had hobbled his ass into the room—still in his Under Armour and unshowered, because who the hell was he trying to impress?—for his ice down.

Rhian's weird behavior would be interesting if it had happened only once. But now, the third time in as many games, it was becoming a pattern.

Henri knew Rhian and Savannah had been friends before they had both come to Boston—Savannah first as the newly hired trainer, then Rhian shortly after as an unexpected call-up when half of Boston's defense was either suspended or injured. Henri also knew Rhian rented the in-law apartment above Savannah's garage in Newton, and that Savannah lived with her boyfriend, Garrick—a nice guy Henri had met a few times at various team functions and games, and who was actually part owner of the team in New Brunswick where Savannah and Rhian had met.

What Henri didn't understand was Rhian's newfound protectiveness. Up until recently, Savannah and Rhian hadn't spent more time together than Savannah did with any of the guys, except that they sometimes carpooled to and from the airport. This week, though, he'd found Rhian having his pre-game nap in the quiet room *twice*, and seen him leave with

Savannah after several of their games. Savannah had to be at the arena long before the players showed up, so it wasn't like Rhian sharing a ride was convenient. In fact, just the opposite, if it meant Rhian had to prepare for their games in a room intended for concussion testing, not naptime.

So why, suddenly, were they attached at the hip?

Savannah turned, just then, and banged said hip against the corner of the counter, hissing as she jumped back and rubbed the sore spot. Rhian twitched, but didn't move otherwise, his gaze still impassive and pinned to Savannah. She didn't seem to notice, as she was too busy glaring at the counter as if it had leaped out to bite her, when, in fact, it was the second time tonight she'd bumped up against it. She'd also almost tipped over her tray a few times, which was wholly unlike her.

If Henri had to guess, he'd think someone's center of gravity was shifting a little. Which, when combined with the way her fleece was a little tighter across her chest—not that he was looking in any sort of inappropriate way—and her face was a touch rounder than usual... well, Henri would bet good money he knew what was going on.

And perhaps why Rhian was hovering so close? Maybe Garrick had asked Rhian to keep an eye on her?

If Henri knew anything, it was that Savannah could take care of herself, and that many pregnant women were not so keen on being coddled. Lisa, his darling diminutive French figure skater and wife, would have strung Henri up by his balls if he'd asked someone to follow her around for one minute during any of her four pregnancies. Savannah was no fool, though, which meant she knew what Rhian was doing and was letting him get away with it.

Henri didn't know what that meant, but he was a nosy bastard—as more than one teammate had woefully noted—and it was going to niggle at him until he figured it out. Not that he'd stick his nose in where it wasn't welcome. But he was observant,

12

and, in his experience, there were all sorts of things he could learn just by sitting back and watching the people around him.

Speaking of which, the bickering in the hallway grew to a crescendo when Jean-Michel accused Noel of being weird—nothing new there, since Noel was a goalie, after all—and Noel shoved them both through the door and into Savannah's office.

Unfortunately, Savannah was standing with her back to the door and didn't see them coming until they'd bumped into her. It wasn't a hard hit, by any means, but she staggered forward, barely catching herself against one of her tables. Before she had a chance to right herself, Rhian was across the room and in Noel's face. Henri didn't know if he'd ever seen Rhian move that fast, and that was saying something, since he was generally considered the fastest defenseman in the league.

"Fucking watch it, guys!" Rhian barked.

Savannah spun, digging her fingers into Rhian's back where perhaps she thought no one would be able to see. Henri cut his eyes away before she caught him watching.

Had Rhian bothered to look back to see the expression on Savannah's face, he probably would have shut his mouth at that point, instead of demanding, "You two need to apologize. And be more fucking careful."

Savannah's knuckles went white where she gripped Rhian's jacket and drilled into his back. Rhian's hands curled into fists.

Henri started to unwrap his knees. Quickly.

Noel and Jean-Michel looked horrified, though Henri suspected neither had any idea of why they were being chewed out by one of their best friends for something that happened virtually every day around the rink. The boys practically lived in this office when they could get away with it. They turned to Savannah for advice about everything.

"Uh, sorry, Savannah," Jean-Michel said, almost like a question.

"Yeah, sorry," Noel repeated, though he kept his eyes on

Rhian. As a goalie, Noel was trained to focus on the real threat at all times.

Savannah jabbed Rhian one more time before she stepped around him to face Jean-Michel and Noel directly. "No worries, guys. It was an accident."

Both boys glanced at Rhian, uncertain.

"What can I do for you?" Savannah asked, her voice bright.

"Uh, nothing," Jean-Michel confessed. He gestured at Henri. "We came to see if Dad was done, and maybe if he and Rhian wanted to go out for drinks."

Rhian glanced at Savannah before turning to gaze out the door over the guys' shoulders. "I can't." He stepped forward, forcing them to part to make way for him. "I've got to go ask Coach something," he muttered before darting out the door.

Noel and Jean-Michel watched him go, obviously hurt.

Henri sighed. *Children.* Like the four he had at home weren't enough to deal with. He hobbled up to Savannah's side. "I think I'm all set. I'll take these jokers out of here so you can finish your work." He turned to the jokers in question. "And stop calling me Dad."

They both ignored him.

Noel turned to Savannah again. "We're sorry," Noel said. "We didn't mean to interrupt."

Savannah waved them off, rolling her eyes. "You're fine. Go have some fun. You earned it. Just don't forget—"

"Protein!" Jean-Michel and Noel said in unison, then grinned.

"We know," Noel added.

Henri put a hand on each of their shoulders. "Okay, guys, help the old man—who is *not* your dad—back to the locker room so we can get out of here." He glanced at Savannah to check one more time for himself that she was fine. "Have a good night, Savannah."

"You, too, Henri."

Henri was feeling magnanimous enough that he didn't even flinch at her attempt to pronounce his name properly in French.

Rhian charged down the hallway, past the locker room, and around the corner as quickly as he could without actually breaking into a run. As soon as he was out of sight of any of the guys still loitering around the arena, he started trying doorknobs until he found himself alone in the janitorial supply closet.

He didn't bother turning on the light, just yanked the door closed and pressed his forehead to the cold metal.

Fuck. He was fucking this up.

He sucked in a deep breath and held it for a second before letting it out. Then he did it again. He kept it up until the feeling of ants crawling over his skin eased and he could roll his shoulders back down from around his ears.

Fuck.

Savannah was being patient with him, but it was only a matter of time before she got well and truly pissed at his behavior. Freaking out on the guys for bumping into her was not what she needed. He knew that. She didn't *need* anything from him, not at work when she was focused on trying to do her job without vomiting. He knew she was strong and that she could take care of herself. That she was never going to do anything that would put herself in danger. But it felt like every minute she was out of his sight—and there were so fucking many of those minutes, goddamn it—something terrible might happen.

He couldn't stop *worrying*.

He felt like his brain had been stuck in fifth gear for the better part of the last month, and the only saving grace was that he was still able to focus on hockey when he needed to. If his anxiety got to the level where it started fucking up his game, then he'd really be screwed.

He took another deep breath, held it for one second, then let it out.

Okay, he needed to chill. He needed to go home and relax. Just be with Garrick and Savannah and be reminded of how much he loved them and that they loved him just as much. It always felt a lot better once he was home. Once they were safe from the outside world and prying eyes.

With a final deep breath, he let himself out of the closet—*ha*—and went back to find Savannah packing up for the night. He hovered in the door, wondering if she'd lay into him the moment they were out of earshot of anyone else, but she just gave him a lukewarm smile and finished up.

Ugh. He'd rather be yelled at.

The ride home was quiet. It often was after a game, win or lose. Savannah was also more tired these days, and she often fell asleep in the passenger seat. Tonight, she didn't, but she didn't say anything either. Mostly she looked out her window, occasionally turning her head to look at him for a few seconds before looking away again.

Rhian thought *he* might be the one in danger of vomiting in the car tonight.

Garrick was stretched out on the couch under one of Savannah's Christmas blankets, half asleep in the gentle glow of the lights on the tree in the corner. He'd barely had the wherewithal to shut off the TV after the game before zoning out, but he snapped awake when he heard the car doors close. He sat up, rubbing his eyes, clearing his vision just in time to see Savannah step into the house and send him a worried look he was becoming all-too familiar with. She was followed by Rhian, who appeared more like a chastised schoolboy than any two-hundred-and-twenty-odd pound professional hockey player should be able to pull off.

Oh boy. Another rough day.

Garrick went to the door to the mudroom and watched as they shucked coats and bags. Rhian didn't make eye contact with either of them as he sorted out his gear, shoving the smelliest of it into its designated closet and tossing the washable stuff through the laundry room door for later. Savannah slid past Garrick to get to the kitchen and he pulled her in to press a soft kiss to her lips.

She felt strong, her grip tight. He wasn't nearly foolish enough to say anything about how tired she looked in spite of that strength. She kissed him back, not quite chaste but nothing too serious, then pulled away and made a beeline for the kettle. Her stomach demanded herbal tea these days. A lot of it.

Garrick turned back to the mudroom. Rhian glanced at him, then up at the ceiling and sighed.

"You want to talk about it?" Garrick asked, not for the first time in the past week or two.

Rhian hovered, looking uncertain for long enough that Garrick began to hope he was finally going to confess whatever had been eating at him, but then Rhian shook his head.

"Not yet."

"Okay," Garrick said, careful to keep any disappointment out of his voice. He took Rhian's hand and towed him into the kitchen, then pulled him close, until their chests bumped and Rhian was staring at Garrick's shoulder. Garrick held him loosely.

"Good game," Garrick said quietly.

Savannah crossed behind Rhian on the way to the cabinet with the mugs. Her hand trailed across Rhian's back and over Garrick's arm on her way. "It was. That goal in the second should have been good. The refs were blind to call the play offsides."

Rhian huffed, but it sounded like he agreed. "I guess we can add it to my pretend numbers. Think they'll let me submit those at contract negotiations?"

"Those aren't for six years, hot shot, but sure. You can keep pretend numbers if you want," Garrick teased.

A hint of a smile curled Rhian's lips.

"Come here," Garrick murmured, and it wasn't possible for Rhian to get any closer, but he understood what Garrick meant.

Rhian turned his head enough to brush their lips together.

Garrick wasn't having that. He leaned in, capturing Rhian's mouth in a proper kiss, one far less chaste than the one he'd exchanged with Savannah, his hand curled around Rhian's neck to hold him still. Not that Rhian was trying to go anywhere. He just liked to be held close. Tight.

Garrick smiled into the kiss when he felt Rhian leaning into him harder, the tension that had held him rigid finally easing away. He wasn't hoping to start anything. He was sure neither of them were—not at this hour, and when Rhian probably needed to refuel properly before he could get some rest.

"Welcome home," Garrick said against his lips.

Rhian kissed him again. "Thank you."

Garrick wasn't sure what he was being thanked for, but he let the kiss linger before separating himself to go into the kitchen to pull out the mountain of chicken and pasta he'd made earlier so Rhian could reheat it.

The proper care and feeding of a professional hockey player was something Garrick enjoyed doing far more now than he ever had when he himself had been one. Savannah liked to tease him about how he took care of them, but he knew she loved it. Just like she knew he loved it, too.

Rhian still seemed, if not shocked, perhaps a little bewildered by the idea that anyone, let alone *two* someones, wanted to take care of him at all. A lifetime in the foster care system, bounced from home to home, had made it difficult for Rhian to accept that Garrick and Savannah really *wanted* to do these things for him. He did accept it, though, and tonight, he took his late dinner with a small smile and another "thank you", without even a *hint* of "you shouldn't have" or "you didn't need to do this, I can do it myself" in the mix.

Reminding himself about how much Rhian had adapted his life to make room for Garrick and Savannah in it soothed Garrick's concerns. Whatever was going on in Rhian's head lately, whatever had him on edge and hovering over Savannah unnecessarily, it would eventually come out, and Garrick and Savannah would be there to help him in any way they could.

In the meantime, they fed him pasta and tea, all the while touching him here and there in the way that made him smile and touch them back. Then they pulled him up the stairs and curled around him in their big bed, pressing him between them until the last of the tension ebbed from his body and he slept.

Chapter Two

Something was definitely up with Rhian, and Jean-Michel was determined to figure out what it was.

For some reason, the rest of the guys on the team liked to rib the French Canadians for being nosy, but that was bullshit. Jean-Michel was just concerned about his friend. That was a good thing! The rest of the guys could take a lesson from him on how to be a good and caring friend.

Also, it drove him crazy not knowing what was going on.

Jean-Michel had a plan, though, and it was elegant and simple.

"Who's up for drinks tonight?!" he shouted to the locker room at large.

The few enthusiastic woos were almost drowned out by the long, low groan of the old guys.

"Come on, fuckers. It's been ages since we all went out, and it's not like we're going to have much time for the rest of the month, with the holidays coming up."

A few heads nodded and Jean-Michel was proud of himself for coming up with that argument. He decided it was time to go in for the kill. He looked to their captain.

"I think we need some team bonding time."

Jean-Michel could see the effort it took for their veteran thirty-eight-year-old captain not to let his shoulders droop. He was cornered now, and he knew it.

He smiled grimly. "Jean-Michel is right, for a change." Jean-Michel squawked indignantly, but his captain continued. "Let's get some drinks tonight, boys!"

This time the enthusiastic whooping drowned out the mutters. Jean-Michel got it, sort of. The old guys wanted to be home with their families and all that shit this time of year. But

20

Jean-Michel needed to help Rhian shake off whatever it was he was carrying around, and he needed the rest of the boys to help him, unwittingly or not.

He turned when someone punched his shoulder lightly. "What's up?" Henri asked quietly while everyone else debated where they should go.

Jean-Michel saw Noel turn towards them, listening from further down the bench as he methodically worked himself free of his gear.

"I don't know," Jean-Michel said. "It just seemed like maybe Rhian could use a night out. He's been..."

Noel nodded, though he didn't look away from untying his pads.

Henri sighed. "You're a good friend to worry."

Jean-Michel preened.

"But maybe you should mind your own business?" Henri suggested.

Whatever. That was pretty rich coming from Henri. If anyone had earned the French-Canadians-are-nosy thing, it was him.

"I don't see how a fun night out with the boys can do any harm," Jean-Michel said, trying and failing not to sound defensive. "You'll see. Even someone as ancient as you will have fun."

Henri rolled his eyes, but his punch stung enough that Jean-Michel smirked, knowing his shot had landed. He grinned at Henri's retreating back and shouted, "I'll see you there at eight, asshole."

Jean-Michel resisted the urge to rub his hands together with glee. Between himself, Noel, and Henri, they could totally figure out what was up with Rhian and maybe cheer him up a little. Everything was going according to plan.

By eight thirty that night, the team had taken over a handful of tables at the back of the pub they'd chosen and were squished into too few seats and booths, just the way Jean-Michel had envisioned. Everyone had a drink and were gleefully breaking their diets for the sake of the best buffalo wings this side of, well, Buffalo. And some of these guys would know, having played there.

Loud laughter burst occasionally from each of the tables, the guys jostling each other over a chirp or to get another wing. You could practically smell the testosterone and male bonding going on all around them. Everyone was happy and having a good time.

Everyone except Rhian.

Jean-Michel sent a desperate look across the booth he'd claimed along with Noel, Henri and Rhian. They'd spent the past half hour joking around and making sure Rhian had a cold beer and good company.

How was that not as close to heaven as a man could get?

But clearly, Rhian wasn't feeling it. He sat tucked into the corner, his hands clenched around his beer, taking slow, methodical sips like it was his job not to actually *enjoy* it. He nodded along with whatever they were saying, smiling when he was supposed to smile, but honestly, Jean-Michel was tempted to check for a pulse.

He was about to just come out and ask what the fuck Rhian's problem was, but the moment he opened his mouth, Henri kicked him under the table. Jean-Michel frowned. What was Dad's problem? And why was he frowning back?

Jean-Michel was saved from having to ask—because subtle wasn't his jam, okay?—when Noel cleared his throat pointedly. Jean-Michel thought he might be trying to back Dad up, but when everyone looked at Noel, he gently tilted his head toward the bar.

"Don't look now, but Rhian has caught someone's eye."

Jean-Michel immediately looked.

Noel sighed. Henri kicked Jean-Michel under the table again.

Rhian glanced at the frankly stunning woman watching him from the bar before dropping his eyes back to his beer.

For a long moment, everyone at the table stared at him, waiting for him to say something. Anything. When it became clear he wasn't going to, Henri cuffed him on the shoulder. "You should go talk to her."

"No, thanks," came Rhian's quick response.

Why the fuck not!?

Jean-Michel didn't say it out loud. He knew that would get him another kick and he had to play a game tomorrow night, which he didn't relish doing with a shin bruised from ankle to knee.

"Not your type?" Noel asked.

Rhian glanced back up, and the woman caught his eye. She was tall, her light-eyed gaze direct, her hair long and so shiny Jean-Michel's hands twitched to touch it, just to see if it was really that soft. Actually, she kind of reminded Jean-Michel of Savannah, only less business-sporty and more bar-flirty.

Rhian's cheeks got a little pinker and he looked back down. "No, she's...definitely my type. I mean, I guess. If I really had one."

Who doesn't have a type?

Jean-Michel also kept that one inside. His shins rejoiced.

"So, you should go talk to her," Henri suggested. He was watching Rhian closely, like this was a test. Jean-Michel had no idea for what, though. He had never been good at tests...

"Nah," Rhian said, and, for the first time that night, took a good, long pull from his beer.

"Dude, you seeing someone?" Jean-Michel asked the moment the idea popped into his head.

He braced for a kick, but it didn't come. Instead, Noel and Henri looked as interested in the answer as he was.

Rhian's head snapped up. "What? No!"

"Then..." Noel said, tilting his head toward the bar again.

"Yeah, okay. Fine," Rhian said, shoving at Jean-Michel and forcing him out of the booth. "I'm just going to go talk to that woman. I mean flirt. Yeah. I'm going to flirt with her," Rhian declared.

He stomped off the moment he was free of the booth, leaving the three of them staring at his back.

Rhian watched the probably very nice and perfectly innocent woman's eyes widen as he stormed toward the bar, then he checked himself, using the excuse of needing to squeeze between tables to slow down and take a deep breath.

It wasn't this poor woman's fault that he was going to have to speak with her. It wasn't her fault his private life was a hell of a lot more private than most people's, and all that left him with was a shit ton of lies and the burning desire to be anywhere but in this bar, approaching some stranger. He felt sorry for her more than anything, and promised himself that he wouldn't lead her on for a second, just for the sake of putting on a show for the guys.

That was why, when he reached her side, he started with, "Hi. I'm not really here to flirt with you, but if you wanted to pretend for a while, I would love to buy you a couple drinks and some wings."

She blinked up at him, her mouth dropping open. He shifted to the left, blocking her face from the view of the back corner and his idiot friends. In hindsight, he recognized he maybe should have eased into that proposal instead of just dumping it on her like that.

Fuck, he was an idiot.

Her mouth was still hanging open, which, remarkably, didn't make her any less attractive, objectively speaking. "Uh..." she stammered.

"I'm sorry. I can also just leave you alone," Rhian offered.

"No, wait." She put her hand on his arm, and he forced himself not to flinch away. Her eyes narrowed on his and he felt pinned in place. Caught. "Let me get this right. You don't want to flirt with me, but your friends are giving you shit, so you came over to see if I would be willing to fake it with you?"

She was kind enough to keep her voice low, so that the people around them wouldn't hear.

"Yes," he muttered, because this was a fucking stupid idea and he was doing it anyway.

"And in exchange for this, I get food and drinks and your company, in a purely platonic fashion."

He could feel his cheeks heating up, but held her gaze. Her smile grew, bright and wide, and it was pretty clear she was laughing at him.

"Yeah, that's pretty much the deal," he admitted. "I didn't want to mislead you, since that would be shitty, and if I flirted for real, I might..."

"Be tempted?" she asked, her smile turning sly.

"No," he said, baldly. Then he felt bad and tried to explain. "It's not you. It's just that I..." Shit, he didn't really have an explanation for this. Not one he could share.

Fortunately, she seemed to get that. She stuck out her hand. "I'm Helena, my friends call me Lena. Nice to meet you."

"Rhian," he replied, taking her hand. "But you can call me *The Asshole.*"

She laughed, loud and bright. Rhian risked a glance over to the table and saw the guys grinning at him. Rhian immediately returned his focus to Lena.

"They seem easily convinced," Lena observed.

Now Rhian chuckled. "They believe what they want to see."

She grinned and put her hand on his arm, leaning in. "Well, we can convince them, provided you were serious about those wings."

"Dead serious. But are you sure?" he asked, his stomach squirming just from having her so close. And touching him. "I can't...it's not..."

"I get it," Lena said quickly, giving him a little more space, but still smiling at him. "You've got a reputation to protect and, perhaps, a secret to keep. You don't need every sports fan in Boston up in your business. Or," she said, glancing over at the table again, "your teammates, either, for that matter."

A fine sweat broke out over Rhian's entire body. *Shit.* She knew who he was. "Hockey fan?" he hazarded.

"Yup," she replied, popping the p. "And, fortunately for you, a discreet one. We're cool. That is, unless you shirk me on those wings. Then I'm calling Pierre McGuire with an exclusive."

The very idea, even though she didn't know shit and he knew she was only joking anyway, made him want to barf. He raised a hand to get the bartender's attention. In two minutes, he'd ordered Lena wings and a drink, and himself another beer. No way in hell he was going back for his partially finished one at the table. He was in far enough over his head as it was.

Savannah curled up on their huge living room couch and tried to focus on the game she'd chosen to watch specifically because New York had a few players that she didn't trust not to try to break her guys when they played each other next week.

This was her preferred way to work from home. She had her favorite snowflake blanket over her legs, her Rudolf pajamas on underneath, and only the television, the apple-cinnamon candles, and the bright, cheerful lights on the Christmas tree in the corner for light.

The boys liked to make fun of her for all her Christmas stuff, but she knew they secretly loved it. Well, okay, Garrick loved it and Rhian was utterly baffled by it, but he did enjoy seeing how

26

happy it made her to decorate their home. She liked to go on and on about those adorable light-up Christmas villages she could hardly resist every year at this time, just so she could see the confusion on Rhian's face as she described the little figurines skating on the little pond with the little cocoa stand.

It was fucking adorable—the Christmas village *and* Rhian's reaction.

She laughed to herself and hoped Rhian was also having a good time tonight. Maybe the boys could get him to cut loose a little. Be less serious for a couple hours. Hell, get him drunk enough to dance, even. She didn't worry that he would do anything stupid. And she certainly didn't worry that he'd cheat. It just wasn't in his make-up, even when it would probably be easier for everyone if he was seen dancing with some woman. Or chatting up someone at the bar.

She was still frowning over that thought when Garrick came back into the room, bearing her a fresh cup of chamomile tea.

"Thanks," she said, taking it from him and putting it on the coffee table to cool.

He nudged her until she made room for him behind her on the long sectional—not that she needed to be convinced. She happily settled herself between his long legs, spreading the blanket over both of them before tucking her side and shoulder against his chest.

She tried to focus on the television again, but was starting to realize she might have to give it up as a lost cause. Her mother had warned her about "baby brain" and now she was getting an idea of what that meant. One second she was watching the TV, the next her eyes were tracing over the heavy evergreen garlands she'd draped along the mantelpiece and wondering if she should add some red berries for color, and then she was staring at the picture of her, Garrick, and Rhian perched among the greens.

"You thinking about him?" Garrick asked, apparently not paying any more attention to the game than she was.

"Yeah," she confessed, turning to look at him over her shoulder. "Do you think he's changed his mind?"

"About us?" he asked in total disbelief.

"About the baby," she said, her heart lodged in her throat from just speaking her greatest fear.

"What? No," Garrick said firmly, pulling her closer. "He's just..." Garrick trailed off, and Savannah wondered if he'd had an idea of how to end that sentence when he'd begun it. "I think he's accepted a lot of changes, and this is another big one, a particularly scary one for him, so I think all that's finally caught up with him," Garrick said.

"What do you mean?"

"Well, there's us, of course. Being in love, *falling* in love with both of us freaked him out. You know that."

Indeed, she thought with a small smile. "Freaked out" was an understatement. But he'd gotten used to the idea. To having them around. Being with them. Living with them and sharing a life.

"And then you add on his discovery of his biological family here in Boston. Finding Seamus and Chelsea, and suddenly having a grandfather and a sister for the first time in his life. Not to mention confronting the mother who abandoned him, and meeting his psycho brother, and *not* having them in his life."

"Thank god."

"Right. Then you throw on a six-year contract, a few million dollars *a year* after a lifetime of having *nothing*."

"And we still can't get him to spend the money," she said with a grin.

"He'll probably have most of it in the bank, untouched, when he retires," Garrick agreed. "So, then you add on a baby, and the fact that he never had a father, and that he's probably worried he doesn't know what he's doing, and..."

"It's a lot," she agreed, getting what Garrick was saying, but finding a new worry in it. "What if it's too much?"

"It's not." Garrick's confidence was absolute. "He's the strongest person I know. He'll figure this out, and when he's ready, he'll come tell us what's on his mind. He will."

"I hope so," she said, but she wasn't as confident. "And before he does something really regrettable at work. He's been hovering."

"You can tell him to back off."

"I'm afraid to," she admitted. "I'm afraid he'll run."

"He won't. He never has."

She turned so Garrick could see her face and the look she was giving him.

"Okay, but that was at the very beginning and doesn't really count. He came to find us to fix it. He's going to come find us on this one, too."

"But we're right here. He sleeps beside us every night. We make love to him, he makes love to *us*. Why can't he just..."

"He will. Be patient."
Savannah sighed, but it was more affectionate than exasperated. "Well, he needs to hurry up." She ran her hand over her belly. "I'm working on a timeline, here."

Chapter Three

Noel let out a deep sigh of relief when Coach blew the whistle and indicated that Noel was done for the day. The backup goalie jumped into the net, getting his shots in for this last part of practice while Noel got a head start to the locker room. Or, more accurately, to the trainer's room.

He almost went in the wrong direction in the warren of tunnels under the ancient arena, but it wasn't his first time in Detroit, fortunately, so he managed without issue.

No issue, that was, until he heard a strange noise and stuck his head through the door to see what was going on.

Savannah was doubled over one of the huge trash cans, her hands braced on either side to keep it from rolling away from her, as she threw up what had to be the entire contents of her stomach. And then some.

Shit, that looked just miserable.

As quietly as he could, Noel snuck back down the hallway and into the locker room. He'd need to see Savannah eventually about what he suspected was the beginning of a tight groin muscle, thanks to the heroic split save he'd foolishly made during shoot-out practice, but he could strip out of his gear and shower first. Give her some time.

And maybe spend a few minutes praying to all that was holy that the food they'd eaten on the flight out here wasn't going to give them all food poisoning. Or that she didn't have a stomach virus, because what one of the team got, they all got eventually.

The rest of the guys filtered into the locker room a few minutes after Noel was done in the shower. He was still sitting on the bench in a towel, consumed with guilt because he should have said something to Savannah and made sure there wasn't anything he could do to help her. It had been pretty shitty of him to have left her alone like that. It was just—Noel always wanted to be left alone when he was sick. And, well, he was squeamish.

Rhian tromped into the room with the rest of the D-corps and smiled at Noel. It was good to see Rhian in a happy mood. He must have had a good practice. But at the risk of ruining that, maybe he should tell Rhian what he'd seen? Rhian was, after all, good friends with Savannah. Hell, he must like her a lot, since he voluntarily lived above her garage, which was just weird—the dude made *millions*, and he lived in an in-law apartment? But whatever, maybe she'd be comfortable accepting some help from him.

"What's up?" Henri asked as he took his seat further down the bench, following Noel's line of vision to Rhian and looking between them.

"Oh, nothing. It's just...I saw Savannah was sick. You know, barfing? In the trainer's room? And I was wondering if I should say something to Rhian."

Noel wasn't sure what Henri would advise, but he sure as hell didn't expect Henri to break into a smile and look so *pleased*. What the fuck was up with that?

And they said *goalies* were weird.

Before Noel could ask Henri what his malfunction was, Rhian wandered over. "Hey. Did I hear my name?"

Noel shrugged and scratched the back of his neck, feeling guilty, again, that he hadn't offered to help Savannah himself. Now, twenty minutes later, it probably wasn't going to do a lot of good, but he plowed on anyway. "Yeah, uh...I thought you might want to know that I caught Savannah being sick when I got off the ice. She looked...well, it looked pretty miserable, man. And I know you two are friends, so—"

Noel didn't bother explaining himself further, since he was suddenly talking to the empty space in front of him. Rhian was back at his stall, ripping the rest of his equipment off like it was on fire.

Noel caught Henri's surprised expression, then they both

31

watched the show as Rhian stripped down to his Under Armour and bolted from the room in nothing else. Not even socks.

Noel grimaced. No one should *ever* walk around these locker rooms without some kind of protection on their feet. That was just *wrong.*

"What the fuck was that?" he asked no one in particular.

Henri huffed out a half-laugh and shook his head.

Rhian knew better than to race into Savannah's office like a lunatic, but he did it anyway. He burst through the door to find her standing in the middle of three of his teammates, calmly discussing their post-practice routines and what modifications were needed that day. The room, and her staff, bustled around her.

She appeared as healthy as a horse as she looked over her shoulder at him standing in her doorway in nothing but a pair of compression leggings—they were tights, if he was being honest—and a long-sleeve t-shirt plastered to his chest with sweat. He probably looked about as good as he smelled.

Worse than being yelled at for being an idiot was the way Savannah kept her face perfectly neutral and asked, "Is there something you need help with, Rhian?"

"Uh...no. I'm good."

The guys were all looking at him funny now. He opened his mouth, but couldn't come up with a single reasonable explanation for his behavior.

"Did you take a wrong turn?" Savannah asked mildly, and he latched on to that.

"Yeah. I guess I did. This old place gets me every time."

He thought maybe a couple of the guys had bought that, and he didn't linger long enough to determine what the rest thought, let alone if he could convince them. Spinning on his heel—his *bare* heel, which was gross, because everyone knew you didn't walk around these places without some form of protection on your feet—he trudged back to the locker room. He didn't make eye contact with anyone—particularly the French Canadian mafia—as he stripped down the rest of the way and ducked into the showers. The bus to the hotel would be leaving soon, and he wanted to be on it and not have to find his own way back. Then, like the fucking adult he was, he could sulk alone in his room.

Road trips were the worst. They hadn't been so bad when Rhian had still lived in hotels full-time himself. The only difference from being at "home" back then had been that the team generally fed him and he was a little busier with all the moving around from hotel to rink to bus to hotel. He'd liked not having to think about much, just being able to do his job to the best of his ability.

Now, though, road trips *sucked.* Rhian wanted to be at home, in his own bed, surrounded by his own things. The idea of having *things* was a relatively new one for Rhian, but he'd taken to it. He'd still, though, burn them all, throw out every object he'd let himself collect, if it meant he could spend all his time with Garrick and Savannah.

But Garrick was at home, and Rhian wasn't. When he'd first signed with Boston for six years, he'd actually thought the travel wouldn't be so bad, since Savannah would be along for the trips with him. Sure, they'd both miss Garrick like crazy, but at least Garrick would have the comfort of home, and they'd have each other.

But it didn't work like that. When they flew, she sat up front with management and worked, while Rhian sat towards the back with the guys and played cards or read. He didn't sleep, almost ever, on the flights because as soon as he closed his eyes, all he did was wish he could move up ten rows and put his head on Savannah's shoulder. It just made the distance between them that much more palpable to him.

And the hotels were the *worst.* Sometimes she'd be a few

33

floors away, other times as close as across the hall—but it didn't really matter which. She wasn't with him, he wasn't with her, and, worst of all, they had to pretend that didn't bother either of them. And maybe it *didn't* bother her. These days she was so desperate for sleep, she probably passed out the minute the hotel room door closed behind her. But he wanted to be on the other side of that door with her. He wanted to watch her sleep and know she was safe and tuck his face against her shoulder and feel her warmth.

Instead, he would be alone in his room, trying to make himself warm with blankets and dry, stale hotel air that would never smell of vanilla and home. And definitely not of Savannah and Garrick.

Rhian hadn't jerked off on a road trip in over a year. That couldn't be normal, could it?

He must have been giving off a pretty good leave-me-the-fuck-alone vibe by the time the team climbed aboard the bus, because even his friends didn't do more than bump his shoulder, then sit down around him. He stared out the window for the short drive, only really starting to pay attention to the world around him when he saw a CVS on the corner. Then a convenience store flew past, just before they took the final corner and pulled up in front of the hotel.

Rhian told himself to chill out and be normal as he followed the rest of the team into the hotel. He couldn't help but notice, though, that Savannah hadn't made the bus. It wasn't all that unusual that she would find her own way back, but when she also didn't show to the dinner the team had arranged in one of the hotel's large conference rooms, Rhian felt twitchy.

He'd already screwed up enough for one day, though, so he didn't run up to her room and beat down the door, in spite of the burning desire to do so. Instead, he slipped his phone from his pocket and checked for a text from Savannah with her hotel room number. They were in the habit of sending their room numbers to each other when they arrived, though usually it only served to make him hyper-aware of how he *wasn't* in her room, instead of offering reassurance that he'd know where to find her in an emergency.

In any case, he had it. And tonight, that *was* a reassurance.

When dinner was over, Rhian begged off joining the guys in "an epic Mario Kart battle" in the lounge that had been set up for them, saying that he was going to go for a walk instead. Henri stared at him, studying him in a way that made Rhian distinctly nervous, but Rhian knew better than to ask.

He smiled fondly at his idiot friends as Jean-Michel rode herd on Henri and Noel all the way down the hall, trying to get them to trash talk about their video gaming skills while they both just rolled their eyes.

Rhian wandered casually out the hotel's front door, but as soon as his feet hit the sidewalk, he turned left and picked up speed. In a matter of minutes, he'd pulled together a bag of Ritz crackers, lemon-lime Gatorade, two Hershey bars, and a tin of peppermints. He found another shop that sold him a box of chamomile tea and two of the largest, cheesiest, glitteriest Christmas mugs he'd ever seen. Savannah would love them. He didn't really strike gold, though, until the appliance store. Loaded down with his purchases, he blended with the rest of the shoppers as he made his way back toward the hotel, a gift-wrapped box with a cheerful red bow under one arm.

He ducked into the hotel's garage entrance, found the elevator, and took it to the sixth floor, where he meandered down the hall toward his own room. When he didn't see anyone, he slipped into the stairwell, then down one floor. He peeked into the hallway on the fifth floor and saw no one, but at this point, he needed to check in with Savannah before he did anything else.

She wasn't going to like it, but at least this way they could prevent anyone else from witnessing his stupidity. That would help, anyway.

He smiled when she picked up on the first ring. "Hi, baby."

"I'm guessing that greeting means you're alone." Just hearing her voice made something in Rhian's chest loosen. "Are you in your room?"

"Yes?" She sounded suspicious.

"Can you let me in?"

"Rhian..."

"I'm looking down the hall. There's no one—"

"Come on. Quick."

Rhian didn't know what changed her mind, and he didn't care much, either. He darted out of the stairwell and down the hall, praying that Coach—or anyone else from management—wouldn't open their doors. Savannah's door opened the moment he arrived, and he slipped inside. She stumbled back a little when he pushed the door wider to get his parcels through with him, but he gladly wrapped his arm around her and anchored her against him as he kicked the door shut.

As soon as she was close, the moment he could feel her body against his and smell her shampoo and feel her hands on his back, he let go a breath he hadn't known he'd been holding.

Savannah frowned down at the numerous bags hanging from Rhian's fingers and the brightly colored box under his arm.

"What have you been up to?" she asked.

"No one saw me," he promised.

"I know you're careful, honey," she said, still eyeing his parcels.

"I wasn't today. I keep messing up. I'm sorry."

Savannah pressed her hands to his back, holding him closer. "You're okay. I mean, yes, you have to stop with the hovering, but I get it's been...that you've been having a hard time with..."

"I just want to know you're okay."

"Well, I am," she said firmly.

"So, Noel didn't see you barfing up lunch into a trashcan earlier?"

Savannah's shoulders slumped. "Oh, damn. I thought I heard something."

"And you weren't going to tell me?"

"What? No. I would have mentioned it to you and Garrick tonight on the phone, if the subject came up. It wasn't a big deal, though. I'm not *sick* or anything."

"You didn't come to dinner."

"Oh, well. Yeah. I ordered some room service." She pointed guiltily at the desk and tray of food she'd barely picked at. The mac and cheese had sounded good when she'd ordered it, but the moment she took off the cover, she'd changed her mind completely.

Rhian passed her one of the smaller bags.

She peered inside and smiled, her heart squeezing tight at seeing the crackers she'd been subsisting on for the last six weeks, as well as a tin of the mints that often helped settle her stomach. Then he reached into another bag and handed over her favorite flavor of Gatorade before loading two more bottles of the stuff into her mini-fridge.

As soon as he stood, she leaned in and pressed her lips to his. He hummed, curling his arms around her until the bags thumped against her butt. She burrowed into his warmth.

She knew, in her heart, that the right thing to do would be to thank him for being so thoughtful, so sweet, and then remind him he had to leave.

She also knew she wasn't going to do it anyway.

"Come on," she said after indulging in the kind of long, lingering kisses that she often dreamed about when she was stuck in her hotel room alone. "I thought I couldn't eat, but now that I've seen those crackers, I'm starving."

He smiled, as if this was all he'd wanted, and her heart hurt with how much she loved him. Then he pulled a box of her favorite tea from one of the bags, and handed her the box. She ripped through the paper, laughing when she uncovered an electric kettle.

"Merry Christmas," he said with a happy grin.

"I don't think I've ever loved you more than at this moment."

She said it unthinkingly. As a joke, almost.

But his face went serious. "I love you, too."

After that, it was just lucky that she got any crackers or tea in her at all, since all she wanted to do was lie down with Rhian and hold him. Have him hold her. She scarfed her makeshift and absolutely perfect dinner, and when he went to make them both a cup of tea, she stripped down, pulled on Garrick's old Ice Cats shirt she used as pajamas while on the road, and climbed into bed.

Rhian looked back at her and frowned before turning his focus to tea-making instead. When he brought her a mug and stood holding his, still fully clothed and looking uncertain, she peeled back the blankets.

"Come on. We'll get you back to your room before dawn and no one will be the wiser."

He didn't move. "Really?"

She sighed, understanding his hesitation, and knowing she should be feeling it herself, but not caring either way. "Yes, I'm sure. And hurry up—all the warmth is escaping."

Rhian was down to his boxer briefs and beside in her in record time. The smile on his face, and the tension she could feel easing from her own body, told her she'd made the right call, even if it sucked thinking about how they couldn't do this all the time. Or, really, at all. Tonight had to be an exception.

With that in mind, she snuggled close, tucked right up under his arm as they called Garrick. He looked surprised to find them together, but he didn't say anything about it, and his warm smile and roving eyes told her he liked seeing them this way. They stuck to their usual subjects—the flight that morning, practice that afternoon, the game tomorrow.

After a series of quiet goodnights and a frankly embarrassing number of "I love you"s, they hung up. Rhian turned off the lights, set his alarm for ass o'clock, then slid down in the bed facing her, their knees touching.

Savannah was tired all the time these days, but she was also sleeping better than she had in ages, so she had some energy left in the tank tonight. She used it wisely, reaching out to draw her fingers down Rhian's chest, enjoying the soft skin and firm muscles as they twitched beneath her touch.

Rhian let out a huff of quiet laughter and disbelief when she curled her fingertips into the waistband of his boxers.

"Really?" he asked.

Her only answer was to kiss him and tug his shorts down over his hips.

They'd been together long enough that this part was...well, easy wasn't the right word. But familiar. And maybe simple. She knew what worked for him. He knew they both wanted it to be quick and quiet. It was only a matter of seconds before her hand was wrapped around his cock, teasing him erect while he eased one of her legs over his hip and tugged her panties aside.

They didn't even have to stop kissing. The awkward days of instructions and needing verbal feedback were in the past. Not that they didn't still revert when trying new things or one of them just felt like telling the other two how they felt or what they were going to do to them. Hell, yes, they did. But tonight, the hum against her lips, the wriggle of her hips, was all the feedback needed.

She'd been thinking about doing this since the second or

third time she'd caught Garrick's eyes drifting down over them both. If she had to guess, Garrick was probably spread out across their bed right now, jerking off while imagining what they were up to. Maybe he was picturing exactly this, her hand running the length of Rhian's shaft and tugging a quiet moan out of him, his index finger tracing exquisite and tormenting figure eights over her clit, again and again.

Her hips twitched against his hand and he smiled against her lips.

She thought about crawling under the covers and sucking him into her mouth, but when she looked down, his fingers threaded into her hair, tilting her head back up and capturing her mouth with his as his hips began to work in time with her hand.

Somehow he managed to do this *while* keeping up a steady, constant flick against her clit.

Goddamn, it was good to be with a professional athlete, she thought with a wry smile that was mostly lost to their kiss.

She circled her palm over the head of Rhian's cock on her next trip up and found it wet, knew it would be going from pink to red as his need grew. She slipped her other arm down between their bodies and cupped his balls, rolling them against her palm as she started jerking him a little tighter, a little faster. He finally lost his rhythm with his fingers, which meant he was close.

Savannah slid two fingers back, tracing along the seam of skin behind his balls, then pressed up hard.

Rhian ended their kiss with a gasp as his back arched and he came all over Garrick's shirt. Savannah stifled a giggle as she looked at the mess. She wished she had her phone handy so she could send Garrick a pic. That would definitely help him with whatever fantasy he was working on, if he wasn't done already.

Rhian took him a minute to regather himself, but once he

had, he smiled softly at Savannah and then meticulously took her apart. She buried her face in her pillow to muffle the sounds he drew from her as his thumb tormented her clit and two fingers pushed deep into her pussy and pressed against her g-spot. She could hear him quietly laughing at her when she bit the pillow, but what else could she do as his pinky wriggled its way into her ass?

Her orgasm washed over her, making her moan as he teased the ripples from her body until she was shaking against him and pushing weakly at his arm.

She slept better than ever that night.

Chapter Four

There was nothing Seamus Lynch loved more than having his family under his roof. Who that included had changed a lot over the past couple years, but only for the better. There was not one ounce of him that regretted having found Rhian and being part of his life.

He smiled, his heart full of love and contentment, as Rhian bickered happily with his sister, Chelsea. No one would ever guess they hadn't grown up together. Maybe there was just something inherent in being siblings. Something that made the fire light in Chelsea's eyes and the devil dance in Rhian's. Chelsea had never had this kind of connection with her other brother, Buddy. Nor with her mother. Indeed, she'd always seemed happiest when she was with friends or with Seamus. And now, with Rhian and his partners, too.

Garrick and Savannah were watching the bickering with similarly fond smiles on their faces, laughing at Rhian's attempt to convince his sister that dating a hockey player would be a huge mistake. He obviously didn't have much of a leg to stand on, since he *was* one, *and* he was dating two hockey players, both of whom obviously adored him. If Seamus had to guess, Rhian's worry was not entirely faked, but he also was putting up the good fight because he could. He wanted to be Chelsea's protective older brother. And Seamus's devoted grandson. And Savannah's and Garrick's doting husband.

In truth, it had taken Rhian a while to get comfortable with these roles, and some days Seamus could still see the struggle. Tonight, Rhian was wrestling with something, though Seamus wasn't sure what. Asking Rhian would be an effort in futility, and Seamus thought he could guess what might be the issue, anyway.

Seamus knew what it meant when Savannah went pale at the mere sight of the pâté and crackers. Pâté that Seamus had

A Merry Little (Hat Trick) Christmas

taken to keeping in house because she liked it so much. Pâté that tonight had turned her positively green when it had come close enough for her to smell. Garrick had been subtle enough in moving it away again, and Rhian had barely tripped over his own feet bringing her a plain cracker and making sure her water was within reach, but Seamus saw. He knew. And it was all he could do to contain himself.

Seeing the guarded way Rhian kept watching all of them did put something of a damper on Seamus's spirits. It had been some time since Rhian had felt the need to be so cautious.

In spite of this, dinner was still fun, the talk light-hearted and without any major announcements, sadly. Chelsea seemed determined to cheer Rhian up, and that did seem to help, but never completely erased the shadows lurking in her brother's eyes. When dinner was over, Seamus sent everyone through to the parlor again, but at the last moment, put his hand on Rhian's arm and held him back.

"What's wrong?" Rhian asked, his look wary.

"Nothing's wrong, my boy. Nothing at all."

"Okay, do you need something?"

"No, not really. I just wanted to tell you..." Seamus realized he probably should have thought about this a little more before diving in.

"What?"

But then again, Seamus knew what he wanted to say. All he had to do was put words to what he felt every time he saw Rhian.

"I wanted to tell you that I'm proud of you," he began, and knew it was overdue by the shocked expression on Rhian's face. He should have been saying this every chance he'd had.

"Uh, thanks," Rhian said, looking pleased but also desperately uncomfortable.

"You are a good man, Rhian. You're kind to your family and your partners and strangers alike. I hope you know that any one of us here would do anything for you. Anything you asked or

43

needed, we would give to you if we could."

Rhian's face fell and he reached out to grab Seamus's arm, startling him. It was unlike Rhian to initiate any kind of touch. "Are you okay?" Rhian asked, his voice surprisingly haggard.

"What? Me?" Seamus asked, confused. Then he realized what Rhian must think. "Oh, no! I'm fine, son. In perfect health still, for which I'm deeply grateful. You'll not be rid of me any time soon, I promise."

Rhian swayed as the tension left his body all at once. Seamus felt terrible for scaring him, but also shamefully pleased that Rhian had been so affected by the thought. He wasn't an easy man to read, and trying to get him to talk about his feelings was akin to pulling teeth, which was precisely how Seamus was about it most of the time, too.

"You're not alone anymore, Rhian. You never will be again. I can't promise to live forever, but you have Chelsea, and Savannah and Garrick. You've built yourself a strong and happy family, and I know you will keep doing that."

Rhian glanced out the door toward the sound of voices coming from the other room. "I will," he said, though the frown on his face wasn't all that reassuring.

"Yes, son, you will," Seamus said firmly. "And we will be with you every step of the way, if that's where you want us."

Rhian turned to look at Seamus. "I do want that. You and Chelsea mean more to me than...I didn't get how it could be, until I met you. How family worked."

Seamus smiled and squeezed Rhian's arm. "I'm glad. I know our family has its issues, to say the least," Seamus admitted, leaving it there in order to skirt bringing up Rhian's mother and brother, "but Chelsea and I love you, and I'm sure the Morrisons offer you ample examples of how a family can and should function."

Rhian managed to keep eye contact when he said in a gruff

voice, "I love you, too," and Seamus couldn't fault him looking away after that. It was just as well, as it gave Seamus a chance to scrub the sting from his own eyes.

And to think, he'd thought he couldn't be any prouder of Rhian.

Seamus cleared his throat. "Yes, well, I just wanted to make sure you knew that. Perhaps now we should join the others."

Rhian did a fair job of not actually leaping through the door, but didn't completely mask how eager he was to get back to his partners and sister.

Once in the parlor, they settled in to chat for a while before dessert. While Seamus hadn't thought the cure for whatever was on Rhian's mind would be Seamus getting emotional on him, he had hoped it would settle him for a bit. It did not. Indeed, Rhian almost seemed worse.

Desperate for a fun topic, Seamus grasped onto the plans for his annual holiday party.

"Did you all send me a list of people you'd like to invite to the Christmas shindig?"

Chelsea said she had. Garrick assured him that his family would love to attend but wouldn't be in the area for the holidays. Savannah, who was curled up in one of the deepest, most comfortable chairs in the room, smiled at him. "I spoke to my family about it, and they all informed me that they'd already received invitations."

Seamus shrugged. "Well, you mentioned they were all coming to town. I hope that's okay."

"Of course! Thank you for being so thoughtful."

Seamus beamed. "It's my pleasure, sweetheart." He turned to Rhian. "And what about you? Do you have any friends you'd like to invite? Everyone is welcome."

"That's okay, I'm good," Rhian said quickly.

"None of your teammates?"

"No. That's okay."

Savannah and Garrick exchanged a look behind Rhian's back.

Seamus persevered. "What about Jean-Michel? Or Noel? Or Henri? I thought you were close to them. I'd enjoy meeting them outside the rink."

Rhian smiled thinly. He managed to sketch a shrug, despite the bow of his shoulders. "Sure. I mean, I guess it won't make any difference if I invite those guys."

Garrick shifted to get a better look at Rhian's face. What the hell did he mean by *it won't make any difference?*

No one else seemed to know what to make of it either, so it hung in the air for a long time before Seamus, a master of keeping the conversation rolling, shifted them all into a new topic.

Garrick resisted the urge to sigh. Rhian had seemed so much happier and more relaxed when he and Savannah had come home from their road trip yesterday. Maybe he hadn't completely shaken the funk he'd been in, but he'd been a lot better. Garrick had figured the night in Savannah's room had helped, though he wasn't clear on exactly why. And now he wasn't sure if the change in Rhian had even been real, or just a figment of Garrick's very hopeful imagination.

Because now Rhian was practically vibrating out of his skin with tension.

Seamus stood. "How about dessert?"

Savannah almost purred. "Yes, please." Her sweet tooth had been cranked to full tilt for the better part of the past month. It was kind of cute, since at work she still pretended she was toeing the line, diet-wise, as an example to her team. The moment she got home, though, she was often found digging in the pantry for the Oreos.

Rhian was clearly putting on a brave face. They always

46

lingered at these dinners, and Rhian was usually the most reluctant to leave. Not tonight.

Garrick stood. "I couldn't eat another bite. That dinner was too good and I overdid it. I was thinking I might take a walk around the old neighborhood. Check out our old building. Rhian, you want to keep me company?"

Rhian leaped to his feet. "Yes. Sure. I mean. Yes."

Garrick barreled through the awkward silence that greeted Rhian's enthusiastic agreement by throwing his arm around Rhian's shoulders and pulling him to the foyer to get their coats, and then out the door.

It was a nice night, cold and crisp, and it smelled like snow, which was fairly overdue at this point in December. Garrick loved how Boston, and the Beacon Hill neighborhood in particular, looked blanketed in snow. At least until he had to drive in it, anyway.

He and Rhian walked slowly along the ancient brick sidewalks, keeping their gazes down to make sure they didn't trip on the uneven surface. It was late enough, and cold enough, that there was almost no one else around, and everyone was bundled up so much as to be unrecognizable, including him and Rhian.

The next time Rhian's hand brushed his, Garrick threaded their fingers together.

There was a moment, no longer than the time it took Rhian to suck in a deep, audible breath, that their hands stayed together, then Rhian yanked his away. He edged further from Garrick on the narrow walk, putting a foot of space between them.

"What the hell was that?" Garrick asked incredulously.

"Nothing."

Garrick was fucking confused, but he knew one thing for certain. That sure as hell wasn't *nothing.*

A sick lump congealed in Garrick's stomach. Up until this

very moment, he'd never once believed that Rhian might want out. Right now, though, that seemed like a distinct possibility.

"Do you...are you thinking about leaving?" Garrick asked, his voice hoarse and barely above a whisper.

Rhian reacted as if Garrick had shouted the question. He jerked to stop and spun toward Garrick so fast he stumbled.

Garrick caught him without thinking, then instantly recoiled, but instead of being rebuffed, again, Rhian grabbed onto his sleeve so hard it made Garrick's arm ache.

"*No*," Rhian gasped, pulling Garrick closer, his eyes wide and terrified. "No...I'm not...*no*. Not ever. I can't believe you—you thought I would *ever*..."

The color drained from Rhian's face, until he was alarmingly pale. He was having a hard time breathing, his chest jerking and shuddering as he gripped Garrick harder, cutting off the circulation in his upper arm.

Garrick grabbed Rhian's other arm. "Take it easy, Rhian. It's okay."

"No, it's not," he said, his voice thin as he sucked in short, sharp breaths.

Garrick searched around them and then shoved Rhian toward the narrow opening between the rows of townhouses. The moment they stepped into the ink-black shadows of the alley, he pushed Rhian against the wall and pinned him there with his entire body.

Rhian looked up at him with wide, damp eyes and Garrick's heart hurt. It had been months, maybe a year, since Garrick had seen Rhian fall apart like this.

"You're okay, Rhi. I love you. I'm right here."

"Do you and Savannah want me to go?" he asked, his voice high.

"God, no. *No*, Rhian. Please don't think that. Not for a minute.

I just overreacted to you not wanting to hold my hand. See, it even sounds dumb saying it. You're okay. We're okay," he said firmly, pressing his face to Rhian's so that their cold cheeks warmed against one another.

"I'm so sorry," Rhian whispered.

"For what?"

"For making you think—for being so weird recently. You and Savannah have been putting up with a lot from me, and I'm sorry."

"It's okay," he said gently, though maybe that wasn't strictly true, given that they'd arrived here. "We know you're working through some stuff. We want to help you, but you have to tell us what's going on. You have to let us in."

Rhian nodded quickly, but remained silent.

Garrick could be patient a little longer, so he refrained from reminding Rhian that they were working on a timeline that none of them could change at this point. They had months—about six, to be exact—but it would be super if Rhian got his shit together long before that.

Rather than pointing any of that out to Rhian, he just held him close. When Rhian stopped clinging to him like a limpet and was just holding on and keeping him close, Garrick tilted his chin just enough to brush their lips together.

Rhian immediately kissed him back and something in Garrick's chest loosened. He cupped his hand around Rhian's cheek and tilted his face up, prolonging the contact. He was running out of ways of communicating to Rhian just how much he loved him. How much he needed him and Savannah in his life. If there were a way to kiss him hard enough, long enough, to make Rhian understand how important his happiness was to Garrick, then he would do that.

In the meantime, this kiss seemed to get some of that across. Rhian's hands shifted over him until his fingers dug into Garrick's hips and his head rested on the coarse bricks behind him as he just gave himself up to it.

It was a start.

Eventually, the cold couldn't be ignored any longer. With a last, lingering press of lips, Garrick pulled back. "You okay?"

"Yeah," Rhian mumbled. "Working on getting better, I promise."

Garrick wrapped his arms around Rhian and held him. "I know you are."

Chapter Five

A good, long, hard practice always went a long way toward settling Rhian. After their night with Seamus and his walk with Garrick, he was surprised he'd slept like the dead, if the dead could cling to two people at once. Savannah and Garrick hadn't said anything when he'd curled into to Savannah and pulled Garrick's arms around them. In fact, they'd both seemed pretty happy about it.

But he kept flashing back to the moment Garrick had asked if he wanted to leave, and it shook him every time.

Rhian did *not* want to leave. And he realized now, more keenly than ever, that he needed to get his shit together if he was going to get through this without irreparably damaging his relationship with the two most important people in his life.

The first step toward that was to stop being an idiot and invite his friends to Seamus's party. It wasn't a big deal. Hell, he should have done it weeks ago. But...

Well, it didn't matter what he'd been thinking. What mattered was that he had to get over his bullshit, and a normal, well-adjusted person would want to invite his friends to what would probably be the nicest party any of them had ever been to.

"Hey guys," he said to the collection of nosy French Canadians hanging around his locker when he came out of the shower. "What's up?"

"You seemed a little off today. You doing all right?" Henri asked.

The fact that his weirdness was finally starting to impact his hockey was all the proof he needed that it was past time for him to get over it. "Yeah, sure. I'm fine."

He got three skeptical looks.

"I was going to ask if you guys wanted to do lunch today," he said, plowing on.

"Okay," Jean-Michel said, always the easiest of the bunch to convince to do something.

Jean-Michel nudged Noel, giving him his best puppy-dog eyes. It was pretty pathetic—but not as pathetic as how quickly Noel caved. Rhian turned to Henri and they both rolled their eyes, lips twitching as they suppressed their laughter.

"Lunch sounds good," Henri said.

"Great, just let me get dressed and I'll meet you guys in the hallway."

A half hour later, they were settled into a booth at the back of one of their favorite restaurants, arguing over whether the spinach-and-artichoke appetizer would be a gross violation of their diet plans, or if they could maybe get away with it if they split it four ways.

"Leave me out of this," Henri said, his hands in the air. "I'm no spring chicken like you three. If I eat shit like that this early in the season, I'll not only pay for it until spring, but I'll feel like shit during the game tomorrow."

"Dude, it must be hard to be so old," Rhian said seriously, trying for a deeply concerned expression.

"You're an asshole," Henri said, equally seriously.

Rhian laughed, glad he'd asked the guys out today. He was friends with these jerks for a reason, and watching Noel try to force-feed Jean-Michel a pita chip reminded him what that was and why it mattered.

They joked through their totally-not-on-the-meal-plan appetizer, and Rhian smiled to himself knowing that later that night, he'd have the pleasure of seeing Savannah's outraged expression when he told her all about it. Then he could tell her that she didn't have a leg to stand on, since he happened to know that she had eaten an entire bag of Hershey's Kisses on Saturday when she thought no one was looking.

When the illicit appetizer was cleared away and his guilt-free salad with extra-extra chicken—there was a reason this place was one of their favorites—was placed before him, Rhian decided it was time to get the whole Christmas party thing out of the way.

"Hey, you guys interested in coming to Seamus Lynch's big holiday party? I can get you invitations, if you want."

Henri stopped with his fork halfway to his mouth. "What?"

"You know, Seamus Lynch? I think you've all met him a couple times. He's a season ticket holder."

"He's the mayor of Boston," Noel said incredulously.

"He is not," Rhian said quickly. "Don't call him that."

"Dude, *everyone* calls him that. The *actual* mayor of Boston calls him that," Noel said. "Come to think of it, the actual mayor of Boston wishes he was invited to Seamus Lynch's holiday party."

"It's not that big of a deal," Rhian said, looking down at his salad and focusing on getting just the right mix of ingredients onto his fork.

Jean-Michel looked at him like he was crazy. "It's not that big—" The table shook, Jean-Michel jumped then bent over to rub his shin.

Henri put his fork down. "How is it cool that you invite us to his party?" he asked curiously.

And this was the part Rhian had been dreading. The part where he had to start lying. "He's a friend of mine."

"A friend of yours," Henri repeated. "It doesn't seem like you two would have a lot in common."

"He's a huge hockey fan," Rhian said, nonsensically. The guys knew perfectly well that a lot of times, those were the kind of people he liked to avoid. Nothing was less relaxing than hanging out with a friend who wanted to pick your team apart.

"Are you sure it's okay?" Noel asked before Henri could poke at it any more.

"Yeah, I'm sure. He'd like it if you could make it," Rhian said, pleased at how steady he sounded.

"Then I'm in," Noel said.

"Me, too," Jean-Michel agreed. "You can crash at my place, since it's walking distance from there," he added to Noel.

Noel shrugged. "Okay. Cool."

Rhian met Henri's eyes and, for a moment, his curiosity over Rhian's relationship with Seamus was trumped by their mutual amusement at the dorks beside them. Rhian wondered if they'd *ever* figure themselves and each other out.

"You should bring Lisa. And the kids," Rhian added for Henri.

Henri's eyebrows went way up. "The kids? Really?"

"Yeah, Seamus loves kids. Loves to have the house full of them, especially around Christmas. He'll have the media room in the basement set up so they can watch a movie, or just pass out on the couches."

Jean-Michel's eyes lit up. "He has a media room? Is that like his own private movie theater?"

It was, actually, a lot like that, but more comfortable and a lot smaller. Rhian wasn't going to tell Jean-Michel that, though. "Why do you care?" he asked instead. "You planning on spending the night watching *Frozen* with the eight-year-olds?"

Henri nodded seriously. "Emotionally, he'd be with his peers."

"Intellectually, too," Noel added.

"In fact, he wouldn't even be that much taller," Henri said in a sly voice. "He'd blend right in."

Jean-Michel opened his mouth to say something, then snapped it closed. Then did it again. And again. He looked like a landed trout.

Rhian had to put down his fork because he was shaking with laughter. Nothing got Jean-Michel more worked up than being made fun of for his height. At six foot even, he was hardly short, but Rhian was six foot two, Henri was six foot four, and they both looked pretty short next to Noel, who was a six foot *five.*

Finally, Jean-Michel managed to spit out, "I can't believe I'm friends with you assholes," which just made them laugh harder. "I am not short, you fucking freaks of nature."

"There's nothing wrong with being vertically challenged," Noel offered gently, patting Jean-Michel on the head. "You don't have to feel bad."

"I'm not vertically challenged!"

"If it helps you feel better, you can believe that," Henri said, then turned to Rhian. "Lisa, the kids, and I would love to come to the party. Please thank Seamus for us. I'm looking forward to meeting him again. He's always been a nice guy when we've met before."

"Yeah," Rhian agreed. "He's really great. I think you'll like him if you get to know him better." And it was true, even if it wasn't really the truth. Seamus was so much more than a great guy to Rhian. It would be nice, though, to have his friends see that for themselves.

"Are you bringing a date?" Jean-Michel asked, and Rhian's good mood dimmed considerably.

He fought to keep his smile in place while he was practically gagging on the urge to say, *"Yes! Two dates, actually!"* They wouldn't believe him even if he were crazy enough to say it.

"Nah, no date for me," he choked out instead.

"No? Is it cool if we bring a plus-one?" Noel asked. He didn't seem to notice the way Jean-Michel stopped chewing and looked at him from the corner of his eye.

"Uh, sure. You seeing someone?" Rhian asked, trying not to glance at Jean-Michel

"Nah," Noel said easily. "I was more asking in case my sister comes to visit me around the holidays. She's been threatening to do it, but won't let me buy her ticket yet."

Jean-Michel's shoulders visibly lowered. Rhian wondered how Noel didn't notice. It was one thing if he wasn't interested in Jean-Michel, or in men in general, but he couldn't be that oblivious, could he?

"That's cool," Jean-Michel said. "It would be great to see Liz."

"You're not allowed to date my sister," Noel warned. He appeared completely serious.

Okay, so apparently Noel *could* be that oblivious. Sweet Jesus.

"I'm not going to date your sister, dude," Jean-Michel said with an elaborate eye roll. "She's totally not my type."

Rhian stuffed a huge bite of salad into his mouth as Henri started to choke on whatever he'd been eating while watching the train wreck unfold before him.

Henri enjoyed watching a good train wreck now and then—who didn't?—but never in his life had he been surrounded by such complete idiots as he was now with his friends in Boston.

Seriously. Eating with these morons was starting to be a health hazard.

He'd been tempted, more than once, to call Jean-Michel out on his blatant feelings for Noel, but then he'd be talking to him about something else, or someone else, or the pretty woman watching him from the pool tables or the super fan who likes to follow him around, and it had become painfully clear that not only was Jean-Michel not ready to talk about his feelings with Henri, Jean-Michel wasn't even *aware* of his own feelings toward Noel.

Well, okay, to be fair, Jean-Michel was probably aware of them, but the poor kid didn't seem to recognize them for what they were.

Which was...amazing, actually. And sometimes hilarious, but other times heartbreaking, like the look on his face when Noel asked if he could bring a plus-one to the party next week.

Good god, it had been painful to watch. And yet, *somehow*, the fucking idiot hadn't put it all together, and Noel wasn't any better.

Noel's feelings for Jean-Michel were a lot less clear to Henri. But then again, Noel's feelings on everything were a lot less clear to everyone. He was, after all, a goalie.

But Henri suspected that if Jean-Michel ever got his shit together, Noel might surprise him.

At this point, though, just about nothing would surprise Henri. Rhian seemed to have a pretty clear view of it, too. Though he wasn't one to talk when it came to being vague and frustratingly unclear about his feelings about things.

Henri had seen the look on Rhian's face when Noel asked if he was bringing a date.

"I've got to head out," Rhian said, standing and throwing more than enough cash on the table. "You guys got this?"

"Yeah, sure," Noel said with a wave.

"Got an appointment?" Henri asked. Rhian often had to be somewhere, but he never said where.

"Nah, just some stuff to do at home," Rhian said.

Henri was singularly unsurprised about the vagueness, but the mention of home was interesting.

"How's things above the garage?" he asked with a teasing grin.

Rhian blinked, a frown flitting across his face so fast, Henri would have missed it if he hadn't been looking. "They're good. It's good. I like living there."

This kid made four million dollars a year. "Cool," Henri said mildly.

He watched Rhian go, ignoring the bickering from across the table, and wondered about what was really going on with Rhian. He'd seemed...better today. Maybe not *all* better, but definitely lighter. Happier. As far as Henri knew, nothing had changed in Rhian's life in the interim between his bad mood and today. Henri was increasingly convinced that it wasn't that Rhian didn't have a personal life, as he liked to pretend. It was that his personal life was private. So private he didn't even share it with his friends.

Henri wondered, not for the first time, if Rhian was gay. It made him sad to think that, if that were the case, Rhian didn't feel he could share that with them. God—and Rhian—knew that Jean-Michel would be in no position to cast any stones. Noel was absolutely not going to be anything but cool with it—anyone who had ever met him would know that. He was cool with *everybody*. And Henri was pretty sure he didn't give off a homophobic vibe either, considering he was himself bisexual, and was the first to call out any idiot in the locker room who forgot what decade they were living in.

Henri wondered, briefly, if it might not benefit all three of his young friends if he told them about himself. Maybe get the ball rolling on an honest discussion between them all.

He'd have to ask Lisa what she thought about that. It was a big move, so not one he was willing to make before he'd had a chance to do a sanity check with his wife.

In the meantime, he'd sit here and try to digest his lunch while Jean-Michel stared at Noel like he'd hung the moon.

Jean-Michel went back to the practice arena after lunch and got on one of the bikes. He'd just eaten, so he wasn't trying to train for the Tour de France or anything, but he needed to burn off some excess energy. Something about lunch wasn't sitting right with him. He'd only been at it for twenty minutes before Savannah popped her head into the gym.

"Hey, what's up?" she asked, her eyes narrowing. If Jean-Michel had to guess, he'd say she was judging his speed. He was probably overdoing it, but she didn't say anything about it. Yet.

"Nothing. Just...you know," he said lamely.

She didn't look like she knew.

But then again, maybe she would be able to help if he told her. She was always good for advice about this kind of stuff. He and Noel would be lost without her.

"Hey, can I ask you something?" he said, trying to figure out if this was a smart thing to do or a possible betrayal of Rhian's friendship.

Savannah came closer and he slowed way down, then stopped. She leaned against the display box for the bike. "Sure, what's up? Is this to do with your training plan?"

"No, that's...fine." Which was maybe less than convincing when she'd just caught him working out when he didn't have to. "It's about Rhian."

Savannah stood up straight again. "What about Rhian?"

"He's been...I don't know. Off? For a couple weeks now, at least. Have you noticed?"

Savannah seemed to think about that for a long time before nodding. "Yeah, I noticed."

"Do you think he's okay?"

"Yes." She didn't have to think about the answer to that at all, apparently.

"Really?"

"Yeah, he's just..." She chewed on her lip for a moment. "He's been stressed about some stuff."

"Is there anything I can do, do you think? Do you know what he's stressed about?"

"No, I don't know," she said quickly.

"Should I ask him?"

"Sure," she said, but she didn't sound sure at all. In fact, she looked extremely dubious.

Jean-Michel sighed. "I want to give the dude his space, you know? But he's been so bummed about something. And I swear he's got no life. I mean, you'd know. He must be holed up in that apartment almost all the time these days, if he's to be believed."

"Yeah," Savannah said, but she seemed distracted by her own thoughts, now.

"Hey, I'm sorry. I didn't mean to drag you into it. It's probably none of my business, but I worry about the guy, you know?"

"No, that's nice, Jean-Michel. He's lucky to have a friend like you."

He shrugged and told himself he had no right to preen under her praise. What kind of friend was he really when he didn't know what was wrong and couldn't do a damn thing to help?

"Just, maybe give him a little time to sort out whatever is bothering him and then he'll want to talk about it," she said in a voice that made Jean-Michel wonder if she believed it.

He nodded, though. "Okay. Yeah, I guess I don't have much choice."

"Yeah, none of us do," Savannah said. She looked at her watch. "If you're done in here, and you promise not to over-do it today, I'm going to head out. I need to get home, I think."

Jean-Michel promised and waved goodbye.

He couldn't stop thinking about it, though. It bothered him through his afternoon swim—which *was* trainer approved—another shower, and all the way home. It was just like he'd said. He didn't have a lot of choice. He couldn't force Rhian to talk, and he couldn't offer to help if he didn't know what was going on. Instead, he'd been resorting to trying to cheer Rhian up. The problem was that he sometimes thought he'd made it worse.

He wasn't an idiot. He'd seen the look on Rhian's face when he'd pointed out the beautiful woman at the bar. The rigid determination in Rhian's expression when he'd gone to speak with her. He'd also noticed the way Rhian's smile had faded when he'd been asked about a date to the party next week.

Jean-Michel thought that maybe instead of pushing Rhian, the best thing to do would be to *apologize* to him.

He called Rhian's cell but got no answer.

The itch under Jean-Michel's skin came back, only now it was bigger.

He called again, and when Rhian didn't answer, Jean-Michel grabbed his keys and left his apartment. Rhian didn't live too far, maybe a twenty-minute drive, and he'd said he had a bunch of stuff to do at home that night, so he should be around.

Jean-Michel stopped at the liquor store on the way and grabbed a six-pack of beer he knew Rhian liked. He'd never been to Rhian's place before, so he thought a housewarming gift of some kind was in order. Not that beer was really that, but it would cover him until he could buy Rhian a fucking plant or something.

So far as he knew, no one had ever been to Rhian's place, and, to be honest, he had never questioned it, since Rhian lived a little further outside the city, and in an in-law apartment, to boot. He also liked his privacy, which Jean-Michel was hoping he could smooth over with some Sam Adams, a winning smile, and an apology.

The only reason Jean-Michel knew how to find the place was because Savannah had hosted a team barbeque during training camp to "make up for being so mean" to them all. Rhian had pointed out his place, and the stairs leading up to it, when asked, but he hadn't offered to give out any tours, and everyone was already entertained enough with catching up with one another.

Jean-Michel pulled up in front of the house and parked, not wanting to pull into the driveway and risk screwing up anyone else's ability to leave. He took a moment to admire the twinkling lights twisted into heavy pine garlands wrapped around the porch railings, and the massive wreath on the front door. There was a candle in every window, making the house look warm and welcoming. There were no cars he could see in the driveway, but all three garage doors—also decorated with wreaths—were closed, so presumably at least some of them were in there and people were home. Rhian looked like he was, given that light shone from every window of his place.

Jean-Michel went around to the back of the garage and jogged up the stairs, which were far more rickety than the fresh coat of paint would lead someone to believe. When he got to the landing, he saw the door was more of the same, without the fresh paint. He frowned at the flecks of blue under his feet and at the old door knob.

Seriously, why was Rhian living here?

Jean-Michel knocked gently, but heard no movement from inside the apartment. He knocked again, more loudly this time.

Still nothing.

Frowning, he leaned in to listen for some sign that Rhian was home, but it was hard to tell if maybe the door was sturdier than it looked, or if Rhian was just being super quiet. He momentarily worried he was about to wake Rhian up from a nap, but it was late for that, so he'd be doing Rhian a favor.

He knocked again, loudly, then put his hand on the knob. He was surprised when it turned easily under his palm. The countless times he'd been accused of being irredeemably nosy ran through his head as he pushed the door open.

He hadn't been sure what to expect of Rhian's super weird apartment, but he was stunned by the sight that met him. The space was one big room, with a cheap kitchenette against one wall, and a door in a corner that he could only assume was to the bathroom.

Other than that, the space was completely empty.

Chapter Six

Rhian paused in the middle of washing the dinner dishes and looked out the window over the sink. He thought he'd heard something in the back yard, but he couldn't see anything. He was thinking about going out to the back porch to check anyway, but just then a pair of arms curled around his waist from behind.

Garrick hooked his chin over Rhian's shoulder. "You almost done here?"

Rhian shook out the last pot and balanced it on top of the rest of the dishes drying in the rack. "Yeah, that should be it."

Garrick's big, warm hands spread out across Rhian's belly and pulled him closer. The curl of Rhian's spine was instinct, tucking his butt up against Garrick's hips as they snugged closer.

"Good," Garrick murmured, his lips brushing the sensitive skin along the side of Rhian's neck. Rhian felt the goosebumps spring to life over that patch of skin and across his shoulders. He tilted his head, stretching his neck for Garrick to reach all of it.

"Starting dessert already?" Savannah asked, amused, from somewhere behind them.

Rhian tucked himself closer to Garrick, so that they were plastered together from shoulders to knees, Garrick's warmth seeping into him, soothing him in a way that nothing else could—except Savannah, of course.

She came to lean against the counter facing him, her fingers tracing gently over his cheek. When Rhian pushed back a little further, Savannah slipped in front of him, so that he was pinned between them. His grip on the edge of the sink was the only thing keeping him and Garrick from squishing her into the countertop.

"Remember the time," Garrick said, his every word another brush of his lips against Rhian's skin, "we had sex with a stick of butter?"

63

Savannah had been just about to press her lips to Rhian's, but now she leaned back and laughed.

"Oh my god, that sounds hilarious—and maybe wrong—when you say it like that!" she said. "And I do remember. I'd have to be dead to forget."

Rhian shook his head. "Wait, you and Garrick had sex with butter, too?"

Savannah put up her hands. "Oh no. That's all you, buddy. But it was back when we still had the deal that Garrick had to tell me everything, remember?"

Rhian could feel the heat rising in his cheeks. He did remember. Vividly.

"He told me all about how you two couldn't even wait for dinner to be finished. That you were so desperate for each other, you used butter to slick up your hands."

Rhian's cock, which had already been enjoying Garrick's attention on his neck, now ached in his jeans. He felt a little dizzy from the rapid shift of blood flow. "Yeah," he said, sounding embarrassingly wistful, "that was fun."

Ever since then, just the smell of cookies baking could get him a little excited.

Savannah reached across the counter and dragged the big butter dish closer. "You want to try it again?"

Garrick went still, and Rhian took a moment to stare at the butter and think. The answer, as fun as that had been, was still, "No."

"Why not?" Savannah asked curiously, without a whiff of judgement or disappointment.

It had taken a long time, maybe more than a year, for Rhian to get comfortable just saying what he wanted. They'd continuously encouraged him to, though, and now he could do it easily. Without shame or worry or even a moment's thought.

64

"We need something better than butter. I want you to fuck me," he blurted.

Savannah's smile was slow and devastating. "Me, specifically?"

Rhian leaned in and kissed her, long and deep, his mind running through the various toys she had in her arsenal that would ruin him in all the best ways. Garrick's hands began to wander, and Rhian was going to have to wrap up any part of this conversation where he needed to be coherent enough to answer questions soon.

"No," he said when he could finally stand to separate his mouth from Savannah's. "Or yes. Whatever you two want."

Garrick's hand on his hip went still, his fingers digging in, anchoring Rhian.

There were nights that Rhian liked to be in charge. Nights when he happily told one or both of them what he wanted them to do and how he wanted them to do it. And then there were nights like this one, where he knew what he wanted, but once he'd put it out there, he was far more content to let his two beautiful and terribly clever lovers figure out the details.

His two terribly clever lovers were also very fond of these nights.

Garrick leaned over Rhian's shoulder and Savannah rose to meet him, their lips catching and lingering. Rhian watched them kiss and counted the beats of his heart each time it knocked against his ribs.

God, he loved them. That he'd made Garrick question that, even for a second, made him heartsore and angry with himself. How had he lost sight of his priorities? Of *them?* Everything he'd ever wanted was right here, in his arms. Everything he'd never dared to hope for, every dream he'd spent his life convincing himself he didn't deserve, was within his grasp, because of them.

He made a noise, something he would deny was a whimper, and Savannah immediately moved to kiss him, while Garrick began sucking on the cord of muscle behind his ear. Rhian's hips moved without conscious thought, rubbing against Savannah's belly and Garrick's thighs.

Those wandering hands of Garrick's landed on Rhian's belt and made quick work of it. It fell to the floor by their feet with a thud. Rhian let go of the counter with one hand just long enough to drop the blinds on the window above the sink. When he looked at the other windows over the breakfast nook table, he realized Savannah must have closed those curtains while he'd been distracted.

"Did you two have this planned?" Rhian gasped as he pressed his lips along Savannah's jaw. Garrick's teeth set themselves to the vertebrae in Rhian's neck, making him shudder.

"I have no idea what you're talking about," Savannah said, completely innocent. Then she reached over and slid open the kitchen drawer that normally held things like cooking twine and the ice cream scoop. But not tonight.

Rhian let out a quiet huff of somewhat appalled laughter.

Clever, clever lovers. They *had* planned this, and he knew why. He wondered if they should talk about that first, but then Garrick's hands coasted over the front of Rhian's jeans and he decided it was going to have to wait. He knew they were trying to help him. To give him whatever he needed. They both understood that sometimes what Rhian needed, what they *all* needed in order to feel whole, to feel *better*, no matter what was bothering them, was to be close.

Emotionally, that was every day. All the time.

Physically, particularly in the midst of the grueling schedule and physical demands of the hockey season, it was a little trickier to manage.

"I want Garrick to be the one to fuck you," Savannah said, because Rhian wasn't the only one who knew how to ask for

66

what they wanted. "But are you sure? There's a game tomorrow."

It was a fair question. A smart one, even, since as a rule, Rhian didn't do this the night before a game because he'd be sore. Tonight, that just didn't matter. He wanted it. *Needed* it. Hell, he even looked forward to the soreness, to the constant reminder of all he had and how fucking fortunate he was. He wanted to sit on the bench in New York tomorrow night and wince every time he shifted, because it would remind him he was the luckiest bastard on earth.

He twisted enough to capture Garrick's mouth for a kiss. When they drew apart, he pressed their foreheads together and curled an arm around Savannah's waist, pulling the three of them as close together as they could get with their clothes still on.

"I want to feel it for days," he admitted.

Savannah's heart tripped in its gallop in her chest.

This was the Rhian they knew. The one they'd been falling more and more in love with for years. She hadn't realized until just now how long it had been since Rhian had asked for what he wanted. Made himself vulnerable with the kind of confidence in his voice that meant he didn't feel vulnerable at all because he trusted them that much.

It had been, in fact, three months.

She was a little sad when she considered the timing, but then he was sliding his hand up her back, holding her closer, and she let that sadness go in the face of a wave of hope that this was the beginning of the end of whatever had been troubled him. They were settling into the season, now. Headed for the holidays and a house full of family who loved Rhian, who would be there to help him ease his worries and answer his questions and remind him how amazing a big family could be.

Savannah had grown up with that, and Rhian had grown to

67

love it as much or more than she did. The poor guy was so enamored with her family, he actually thought her nosy brothers were charming. He'd get over that, eventually.

In the meantime, she put away thoughts of family and focused instead on the two men before her. The first thing that needed attention was all the clothing—it had to go. She nudged at them until they were facing each other, lost in what looked to be long, heady kisses, while she went to work on their buttons and zippers. When she'd opened everything she could, she stepped back.

"Strip."

They did, dropping shirts and jeans on the floor around them, then tugging her shirt and yoga pants off, too. When they were all naked, Garrick kicked the entire pile into the corner to be retrieved later.

Then he turned to Rhian and cocked one eyebrow. It was Rhian's chance to change his mind, but instead he just smiled and reached into the open drawer for the bottle of lube.

When his fingers bumped into the other contents of the drawer, he turned to give it a proper look.

"Jesus Christ, did you bring the entire contents of our bedside table downstairs?"

"Not even close," Garrick said with a smirk, tugging the bottle from Rhian's hand. "And there are some new things in there, too. Some early Christmas presents for you."

Rhian leaned in to get a better look and Savannah took the opportunity to run her hand down his side and over his gorgeous butt. She dug her fingers in, enjoying the give of firm muscle and soft skin.

Hockey butt was a real and wondrous thing. Seriously.

Rhian clung to the counter and the drawer, letting her do as she pleased. Based on the way his head hung from his shoulders and his toes curled against the hardwood floor, he was pretty happy with it, too.

He jumped when Garrick drew a shiny finger down the valley of his ass and tucked it against his hole.

Rhian let out a long sigh. Savannah almost giggled at the sound as she helpfully pulled his cheeks apart, watching Garrick circle the pad of his finger over tightly clenched muscles, pressing to ease them until his finger slipped into Rhian.

Rhian muttered a short, sharp, happy noise.

Savannah silently checked with Garrick, who nodded before tilting his head toward the drawer. She nodded back.

Rhian had been right. They did have a plan. Though the previous iteration had included convincing Rhian to break his rule about sex before a game, as he only did a few times a season. Clearly, he was way ahead of them there. They still had a few tricks up their sleeves, though.

Savannah had been thinking about it since the night in the hotel in Detroit with Rhian. He'd held her against his chest the entire night, clinging to her long past the hour when they might usually roll apart to spread out, or at least change position. He hadn't seemed interested in, or maybe capable of, letting her go.

Rhian often drew reassurance from physical contact in a way that Garrick and she rarely needed, and they wanted to make sure Rhian got that. Got everything he needed. She'd thought about it a lot since Detroit, and how little time they'd had since the start of the season to really spend paying *intimate* attention to each other. They still had sex, of course—but they hadn't really taken their time. It hadn't been on purpose, and hadn't had anything to do with the pregnancy. It had just been...timing.

Bad timing that needed to be corrected. And the best way to do that was to make up for lost time and absolutely take Rhian apart. She was sure it would make all three of them feel better.

They'd start in the kitchen, and maybe end up in the bedroom. Or maybe not. She'd learned long ago these plans were best left as general ideas so the rest could unfold as it would.

She slid her hands around Rhian's ribs and ducked under the arm braced against the drawer so that she could press herself to his chest and pull him down for a long kiss. He let go of the drawer to hold onto her instead and she held him steady, shifting with him as his hips jerked and pushed back against whatever Garrick was doing.

When she pulled back from the kiss, Rhian kept his eyes closed, just breathing and running his hand up and down her back. Savannah took advantage of the opportunity to reach behind her and fish the smallest of the butt plugs from the drawer.

It was maybe an inch and a half at the widest point, less at the narrower neck that would hold it inside him for a while until Garrick was ready to take the next step. Neither of them was in any hurry. She held it out and Garrick immediately plucked it from her fingers. Then she just watched Rhian's face, smiling at the blissed-out expression and how it shifted when Garrick did something Rhian particularly liked or wasn't expecting. Or both.

She knew the moment Garrick pulled out his finger, or fingers, by Rhian's frown. Then his eyes popped open and he looked right at her.

"That would be the plug," she guessed with a grin.

Rhian nodded, his mouth falling open, his gaze losing focus until a great shudder ran through him and he stood up.

"Your turn," he said, his voice rough.

She squeaked when he wrapped his hands around her waist and plucked her up off the floor like she weighed nothing. Her flailing hands landed on the kitchen island a moment before her ass did. Then she burst out laughing, because he was ridiculous—and because the granite slab was freaking *cold*.

She squeaked again as she was dragged to the edge of the counter, her hands clutching the edge for dear life as Rhian lifted her knees and draped them over his shoulders.

She barely had time to register his smug smile before he bent over and pressed his lips to the sensitive skin of her bare mons. His evening stubble tickled and she squirmed, shamelessly spreading her legs. She trusted his fierce grip on her hips to anchor her as she opened herself to him.

The first brush of his tongue against her clit made her shudder so hard, she almost slipped from his grasp. Rhian paused, glancing up at her.

She leaned back on her elbows on the freezing granite and kicked his shoulder, "Don't you dare stop now."

Rhian grinned, then pressed his smile against her, his curved lips tickling along her labia, followed closely by the warm, soothing velvet of his tongue. Electric sparks shot up her back, warming her in spite of the cool rock beneath her. When she sucked in a deep breath, it came back out as a low moan.

God, he was good at this.

Good enough to make her mostly forget about the hard surface she lay on. She briefly considered suggesting that they move this to the couch in the living room, but then noticed that Rhian was bent in a way that was pretty much perfect for the next step of the plan. And if Garrick's expression or the steady shifting of Rhian's hips was anything to go by, that was still working for everyone.

Savannah stared vaguely down the long, strong expanse of Rhian's back, admiring the shift of muscle and glow of flushed skin, then looked up to meet Garrick's eyes. It was hard to focus, but she wanted to see. To watch Garrick take Rhian apart. Even if Rhian was doing his level best to melt her brain.

His attention on her was relentless, but he still jerked in reaction to Garrick's hand brushing over the curve of his ass. Rhian sucked her clit into his mouth just as Garrick grabbed the base of the plug and tugged, which translated to a mind-bending level of suction against the bundle of nerves he held between his lips. She writhed against him, using her legs to urge him closer, even though that was impossible.

The expression on Rhian's face was one of utter contentment, like he could happily stay like this, with them, for hours. She watched, fascinated, as Garrick's biceps shifted and bulged, and Rhian's hips rolled back in response. She knew the moment Garrick stretched Rhian open by the hint of teeth scaping across her clit.

Savannah squeezed her eyes shut, spreading her legs further and grinding up against Rhian's face. He shifted lower, thrusting his tongue into her, licking and sucking along her labia until her every exhale came with a groan. Her breathing was getting hectic, her face hot. When she opened her eyes again, Garrick didn't look much better, his cheeks red as he stared down at whatever he was doing to Rhian.

She didn't see Rhian's shoulder's shift, not realizing what he was up to until his lips clamped over his clit again and he pressed two fingers high inside of her.

Savannah's elbows shook beneath her and she gave up, stretching out on her back on the counter island and reaching over her head to clamp her hands around the far edge, using that leverage to push herself down against Rhian's lips.

He thrust his hand so fast it must have been a blur, just the way she liked it, and she rode his fingers happily, one foot slipping on the ball of his shoulder, the other skidding down his spine when she arched her back.

She was close. So close.

And then she was there.

"Rhian!" she shouted as her spine arched high off the countertop, her legs shaking and hips thrashing against him. The waves crashed over her and he pulled more from her with the pulse of his lips and the thrust of his fingers. She threaded her fingers into his hair, just about to grab hold and tell him to stop, when his head snapped up and he gasped.

"Oh, fuck," he moaned, his eyes fluttering closed, his neck arched, his entire body rocking forward against her. Garrick's eyes widened, and Rhian's fingers dug into her thigh so hard they were sure to leave bruises, but for a moment she couldn't comprehend what was happening.

Then Rhian slumped against her, all the air leaving his lungs at once.

"Holy shit," she said, looking up at Garrick. "Did he just come?"

"Untouched," Garrick said with wonder and something like pride.

Rhian groaned against her thigh. "I don't know if you can call it that."

"I never once touched your dick. All I was doing was playing with the plug."

"Oh, is that all?" Rhian said dryly, pressing a goofy grin into her thigh.

Savannah snorted, then propped herself up on one arm and ran her fingers through Rhian's hair. "You okay?"

"Yup," he murmured, sounding utterly satisfied. "I'm sorry I went off too fast. When I'm not semi-unconscious, I'm going to be embarrassed about that."

Garrick ran his hand up and down Rhian's spine soothingly. "Hey, don't worry about that shit. Just stay right there, okay?"

"Okay," Rhian said with a happy sigh, and Savannah could tell by the weight on her leg that he wasn't close to thinking about standing, or even lifting his head.

Garrick reached into the drawer and pulled out another, bigger plug. Savannah barely swallowed back her guffaw at seeing the garish candy cane stripes decorating the substantial toy. The fact that it was vaguely shaped like a tree really added to the Christmas spirit, she thought. She watched, grinning, as Garrick carefully lubed it up and put it aside where he could reach it. When he tucked his fingers around the anchor to the plug still in Rhian, Rhian didn't so much as flinch. The only sign he felt anything was his long, shuddery exhale as Garrick pulled it out.

Garrick immediately slid two fingers into Rhian. Deep.

"Fuck," Rhian moaned softly. He had to be so sensitive now.

"Does that feel good, baby?" Garrick asked.

"No. Yes." Rhian shook his head. "I don't even know."

Garrick drew his fingers out slowly, then thrust back in. Rhian hummed. Savannah smiled at how content he sounded. She saw Garrick twist his wrist, so she was prepared for Rhian's grunt of surprise and full-body jerk.

"What are you doing?" he gasped.

Garrick smiled. "Getting you ready."

"For what?"

"You said you wanted me to fuck you."

Rhian's head finally came up off her leg, his expression confused. "But I already..."

Savannah could see from the angle of Garrick's wrist and the way that confusion melted off Rhian's face that Garrick was rubbing over his prostate relentlessly. The flush returned to Rhian's face, spreading down his neck to his shoulders and chest. He groaned and gripped Savannah's thighs tighter. She couldn't tell if he was succumbing to pleasure or agony, and she didn't think Rhian knew either.

Rhian never looked at the new plug resting by his hip, nor did he seem to notice when it disappeared.

He definitely noticed, though, when Garrick's pulled his fingers away and pressed the blunt end of the plug against him instead.

Rhian went rigid for the span of two seconds, then he pressed his face to Savannah's belly and went lax, giving a little nod. She ran her fingers through his damp curls while he rubbed his face against her. He was probably noticing again how much firmer it felt, and not in a toned-muscle kind of way. It had only just really begun to change at all, and she loved it.

Rhian placed a row of soft kisses across her skin while she and Garrick watched. She twisted her fingers in his hair and he rolled his head to look up at her. His green eyes were hazy, his expression warm and full of affection.

"I love you," she said.

"I love you, too."

Chapter Seven

Garrick pressed his lips between Rhian's shoulder blades and just enjoyed how happy Rhian looked with his head resting on Savannah's belly. He caught Savannah's gaze, and she looked more joyous than he'd seen her in weeks.

They were all right. They were going to be better than all right.

This family was going to be awesome.

With a final press of his lips, Garrick stood and stared down at where his hand held the thick plug against Rhian's ass. The first third had slipped in without any resistance, which had been ridiculously hot. It also meant Rhian would be relatively comfortable, once they got through the tricky part of getting the widest bit past his sensitive rim.

That was, though, a really tricky part. Fortunately, Rhian would love every minute of it.

Garrick twisted his wrist and Rhian twitched when the plug glanced off the right spot. Garrick took advantage of Rhian's distraction and pressed forward.

He didn't expect Rhian's body to open up and accept another third, but it did, just like that. Rhian groaned, the sound muffled against Savannah's skin.

"That a happy sound?" Garrick asked, needing to be sure.

"God. It is. I don't know why it is. I should be kicking you."

Garrick nudged the plug forward, then eased back, taking up a steady rhythm of gentle thrusts and slow retreats. He ran his finger along Rhian's rim, marveling at how it stretched taut. He regretted not having used a lube that didn't taste like hell.

Of all of them, Rhian enjoyed this the most. He liked having his ass played with, would happily submit to it for hours over the summer. Maybe that was because for a huge portion of the year it just wasn't possible. In theory, it shouldn't have been possible now, but Rhian had seemed certain and Garrick was never going to say no to either of them.

He pushed the plug a little harder, a little further, and Rhian grunted. But he also leaned into Garrick, his body stretching beautifully to accommodate the plug.

"Jesus Christ, how big is this thing?" he groaned.

Before Garrick could answer, he gave a last nudge and the plug slipped into Rhian's body and seated there, the anchor lodged tightly between his cheeks.

"Jesus *fuck*," Rhian gasped, his hands spasming around Savannah's hips, but Garrick knew it wasn't a complaint.

He smiled and tucked his hands under Rhian's ribs, urging him to stand.

"What...are you...oh my god."

Rhian waivered on his feet in the middle of the kitchen, naked as the day he was born and more beautiful than any other man Garrick had ever laid eyes on. Garrick kept his hands on Rhian to steady him—or to catch him if needed—but also just to feel his warmth and register the steady, if rapid, beat of his heart.

"How's that?" Garrick asked playfully.

"Umm...wow."

Savannah sat up on the countertop. "Ready to head upstairs?"

"What?" Rhian asked, shaking his head. His hand hovered by his hip, as if contemplating reaching behind him to feel the plug for himself.

Garrick threaded their fingers together instead. "Yeah, let's head upstairs."

Rhian looked adorably confused. He shifted to glance at Garrick over his shoulder, then froze. "Jesus Christ."

"You all right?" Garrick asked, grinning.

"It's...it's right there. On my...fuck, this thing is really well designed," he concluded, shifting again, this time with intent.

Savannah laughed and jumped off the counter. Rhian may have been a little lost in his own head, but he wasn't so far gone that he didn't reach for her, making sure she was steady on the landing.

When she turned to get their clothes from the corner, Rhian let his hand trail along her belly.

Savannah smiled. Garrick had to kiss him.

Goddamn, this was a good idea.

He pulled Rhian flush against him, one hand low on his back, the other pressed between his shoulder blades. Rhian leaned up until their lips met, his eyes fluttering closed as Garrick's tongue slid over his. Garrick's cock, which had gone neglected for so long now it had started to ache, was pressed between their bellies. Rhian twisted just a little in his hold to rub against it.

Garrick shivered and rolled his hips, dragging the sensitive head along the ridges of Rhian's firm abs on one side, and Garrick's admittedly less firm stomach on the other.

He broke their kiss with a gasp. Rhian leaned forward, as if to chase him, but Garrick stopped him with a firm grip around one ass cheek. Rhian jerked to a halt, then swayed where he stood.

Garrick massaged the muscle beneath his palm, forcing the plug to shift over and over. He was so thoroughly enjoying the expressions chasing across Rhian's face, he almost didn't notice Rhian's growing erection until it brushed against his thigh.

"God, I wish I was still in my twenties," Garrick muttered, stroking the thickening length.

Savannah laughed and swatted him on the butt. "Come on, you two, before you get any more distracted."

Which was fair, really.

Garrick was tempted to walk to the bedroom without

relinquishing his hold on Rhian's cock, but as soon as he stepped away, tugging on Rhian's shaft in the process, Rhian's knees wobbled.

Garrick let go of Rhian's dick and slid and arm around his waist instead. "You going to be able to get upstairs?"

Rhian nodded, his lower lip caught between his teeth, his eyes pinned to the floor as if he needed to watch where he put each step.

Garrick stayed close, holding Rhian steady on the stairs. As soon as they were safely on the landing, though, he let his hand wander, tracing over skin and muscle until it landed against the plug's anchor and he gave it a little tug.

Rhian caught himself on the door frame. Garrick expected to be scolded, but instead Rhian moaned. "Jesus Christ, this thing feels amazing."

Garrick ran both hands over Rhian's ass, watching through the door as Savannah chucked all their clothing into the hamper and came back to them.

She cupped Rhian's cheek and turned his head until he could kiss her.

Rhian wriggled his ass and Garrick took the hint, grabbing the plug and tugging on it again. Rhian's rim bloomed around the thick bulb and it was Garrick's turn to get a little weak in the knees.

If he didn't fuck Rhian soon, he was either going to come the moment so much as a breeze blew past his dick or die of blue balls.

"Come on, in you go," Garrick said hoarsely, with a pat to Rhian's butt.

Rhian staggered through the door and to their enormous bed, then waited there instead of climbing up onto the mattress.

"You okay?" Savannah asked with a grin that said she knew he doing a lot better than that.

"If I sit down, I'm going to come again," Rhian admitted,

almost sadly. He waved his hand at waist height and everyone's eyes dropped to Rhian's erection. The head was red and shiny with precome, the shaft riddled with veins where it stood away from Rhian's body.

Garrick almost felt sorry for him, but he was too busy wishing he was in his twenties still. At least having a lover who was sure did have some advantages.

Savannah took mercy on Rhian and climbed onto the bed, towing him with her so that they knelt facing each other. When Rhian sat back, he spread his knees and kept his heels far enough apart that they dug into his buttocks, leaving the plug relatively untouched.

Or, it was until Garrick slid onto the bed behind him, framing Rhian's thighs with his knees, and reached down to tug the anchor again.

Savannah swallowed Rhian's gasp as she kissed him. He clung to her while he licked into her mouth and her hands tangled in his hair. He moaned, the sound a low vibration in his chest as Garrick began working the plug against his rim, not quite pulling it out, but stretching him over and over.

A sheen of sweat popped up across Rhian's skin and Garrick tasted it on his neck and along his shoulders. Rhian hung there between them, letting them do as they wished, letting them know with a thousand little movements and sounds that he was happy. They didn't need words, and eventually, even the sounds stopped, except for Rhian's panting breaths. He was barely holding himself up as he traced his lips along Savannah's jaw and down over her chest. She knelt higher and he licked along her solar plexus and under the heavy weight of one breast, until her fingers tightened in his hair and she guided him to her nipple.

Rhian hesitated there, looking up to see her face above him. "Are you sure?"

She smiled. "Let's try it and see."

Garrick watched as Rhian drew Savannah's nipple into his mouth. It had been nearly two months since they'd stopped doing this, stopped touching her breasts almost completely when they'd become so sensitive she couldn't stand any stimulation. Now they were rounder, fuller, and the moment Rhian's cheeks hollowed, Savannah crushed his face to her chest and moaned.

Fuck. Garrick wrapped his fist around his dick and clamped down.

Rhian sucked harder.

"Oh god, Rhian. That feels so good." Savannah swayed on her knees.

Rhian switched to the other breast, holding her close as he licked and nipped and she gasped and wriggled.

"Fuck, you need to suck. Please...yes, like that, *god,*" Savannah cried, her breath coming in short, sharp pants.

Garrick's head spun in sympathy as Savannah reached down to run her fingers over her clit. Bright red seeped into her cheeks, her eyes gone sightless, and he realized she was close to orgasm. From having her breasts sucked, which had never come close to having this effect on her before.

Rhian must have realized it, too. He hooked an arm around her waist and another behind her knees, scooping her up and letting her fall on her back on the bed. Then he was over her, his mouth latching onto her again, working from one nipple to the other as his hands ran down her body and hoisted her thighs up to hug his ribs.

Shit. Garrick shook himself out of his stupor. He needed to get back into the game before the game left him behind.

Rhian hovered over Savannah, supporting himself on his elbows and knees, his cock hanging heavy above the bedspread, leaving darker spots when it brushed the bunched-up material. His knees were spread wide, the bright red and white of the plug base stark against his pale skin. Savannah thrashed in his arms, arching her back to shove her breasts closer to his mouth, harder against his questing teeth and lips.

Garrick dove for the bedside table and grabbed a bottle of lube, then crawled behind Rhian and seized hold of the plug, noting the way Rhian canted his hips up, begging him to just do it.

He pulled. Once. Hard.

The bright candy-cane colored plug popped out of Rhian and fell to the bed with a heavy thud.

Jesus Christ. And merry fucking Christmas.

Garrick's hands shook as he dumped probably way more lube than he would need over his dick. He made a cursory pass with one trembling hand to spread the slick around evenly.

In all that time, Rhian never clenched, staying open and ready in a way that Garrick had never seen before.

Garrick was a big guy, in general, and his dick wasn't exactly slender or short. He wasn't going to be signing up for any contests, but when a guy was six foot five and built to carry over two hundred and twenty pounds and still be lean, his proportions were just...bigger.

For that reason, Garrick tended to go slow at times like these.

Tonight, though, he lined himself up and thrust once, all the way in.

Rhian's head came up, his mouth leaving Savannah's nipple with an obscene pop, his neck stretched in a long, gorgeous arch as he shouted a series of increasingly filthy words, mixed in with Garrick and Savannah's names.

Savannah, sprawled and panting on the bed, stared up at Garrick with wide eyes. Garrick tried to smile back, but it wobbled badly. He felt feverish with the need to move, to push farther into Rhian and make him feel every inch, every ache soothed, and every need fulfilled. Rhian clenched around him,

82

hard, and Garrick ground in, curling over until his head rested between Rhian's shoulders and he could feel how the muscles in Rhian's back quivered as he held himself still.

"God, I love you," Garrick muttered against Rhian's sweat-slick skin.

"I love you, too," Rhian practically sobbed. "I love you both. Please, you have to know that."

Savannah ran a hand over Rhian's cheek and down to his shoulder. "We do know."

"I'm so sorry," Rhian whispered, his voice hoarse. "I'm so, so sorry. I need to talk to you. About something. It's not...it's okay, though. You have to know how happy I am to be with both of you."

"We know, Rhian," Garrick said, lifting his head. Rhian wasn't one for babbling, particularly not at moments like this.

They'd meant to take him apart. Now, Garrick was worried they'd broken him.

When Garrick rose up, Rhian shifted back with him, seating himself firmly on Garrick's dick, not letting a millimeter of him escape.

"Easy, love," Garrick murmured, running his hands down Rhian's sides. "We've got you. We're not going anywhere."

"I know." Rhian shifted and Garrick moved with him, his eyes crossing at the pressure and friction as Rhian planted his knees more firmly and rose on one arm. "And I've got you," Rhian said as he curled his other arm around Savannah and yanked her down the bed until she lay underneath him.

She yelped, then laughed, until, with a swivel of his hips that dragged Garrick right along with him, he slid into her body and her laughter was choked off with a long, low moan.

"God, Rhian," she sighed.

Rhian didn't answer, but perhaps that was because his mouth was full again. He had pulled one of her nipples into his mouth, his cheeks hollowing with how hard he sucked, and

Savannah cried out, arching up against him.

Garrick thought that was probably his cue to move. He pulled back, his entire body shuddering at the tight clench of Rhian's body, then he shoved back in.

His last coherent thought, other than that he loved these two beautiful people more than he'd ever thought was possible, was that he probably shouldn't have encouraged Rhian to come once already, because there was no way in hell Garrick was going to last.

Rhian wasn't going to last. It was insane—and improbable, given that he'd just come a few minutes ago in the kitchen and, in spite of what Garrick said, Rhian wasn't *that* young anymore.

But he could feel the tension curling up his spine, tightening the muscles in his ass and back and hips. Garrick was so far in him, so deep, that it felt like he was snugged up against Rhian's diaphragm, forcing the air from his lungs with every shift or thrust. The stretch was exquisite, the burn lost entirely to the thrills running up and down his spine. The hot, wet clench of his beautiful, sweet Savannah around his cock was perfect.

As soon as Garrick had a steady rhythm, each thrust growing just a little more powerful, Rhian forced himself to relax so that his body would shift with each plunge to thrust into Savannah. She groaned at the drag, the friction, but it seemed less important than whatever was going on with her breasts.

Rhian was really a big fan of Savannah's breasts, as a rule, but this was something else. She had never been this responsive, this sensitive, before. And Rhian was enjoying the hell out of it.

Also, he was definitely changing his rules about not having as much sex during the season. Garrick felt fucking amazing, and Rhian couldn't help but change things up, shoving back to meet each thrust, then rocking forward into Savannah and forcing Garrick's long, thick shaft to drag against his rim even quicker.

On his next shove back, he met Garrick's hips with enough force that the slap was audible above their moans. Rhian cried out, then rocked forward, meeting Savannah with less force—and noise—but no less pleasure.

God, he was almost there.

He might have said that aloud, because Savannah groaned and clamped down around him, while Garrick shifted, the bastard, and absolutely nailed his prostate on the next thrust.

Rhian shook all over, barely able to retain enough coordination to keep moving his hips between them.

"Come on, baby. Do it," Garrick growled, thrusting again.

Rhian almost shouted, "I'm trying!" but bit down on Savannah's nipple instead. She howled, then twisted against him, trying to change the angle of his thrusts.

He wasn't really in any position to help, but he tried, forcing his hips to go faster, dragging his cock along her soft walls as fast and as hard as he could, all the while doing the same to himself on Garrick's cock in his ass.

His heart was beating so hard he thought he might die. Then his heart stopped altogether as two things happened at once.

Savannah reached down between them and flicked her clit maybe twice, then let out a mighty scream that would ring in his ears for days and clamped down on his cock so hard he saw stars.

And Garrick slid a finger right beneath his cock into Rhian's already stretched hole and pressed down on his prostate like it was a fucking power button.

Rhian's orgasm roared over him like a tidal wave, whiting out his vision, blanking out his ears so that all he could hear was his own hoarse shout and the buzz of a million neurons doing a happy dance.

He thrashed against Garrick, making the burn and the stretch worse. Better. Garrick pulled his finger out, clamped down on both of Rhian's hips to hold him steady as he ground against him. When Rhian's senses came back online, all he could hear was Garrick telling him, again and again, in a ragged voice, how much he loved him. How beautiful he was. He could feel Garrick's cock pulsing in him as Garrick's hips twitched against him. Just when the pleasure might have turned to pain—because there was no way in hell he was going for a third round tonight—Garrick pulled out.

Based on the desperate gasp of breath and the bounce of the bed, he may have actually collapsed back there.

Rhian didn't dare turn to look. He held himself on trembling arms and stared down at Savannah. She smiled, kissed him gently once, then slithered out from under him. The moment she was clear, his arms gave out and he face-planted on the bed.

Savannah ran her hand down his side and he stared up at her blearily through one eye.

"You okay?" she asked.

Garrick dragged himself to sit beside her, his hand joining hers along Rhian's ribs.

Rhian didn't yet have the higher brain function necessary for things like speech, so he smiled weakly instead. He could feel Garrick's come sliding out of him, and he thought this just might be the most content he'd felt in...god, months. Ever, maybe.

But then, he'd had that last thought before. Savannah and Garrick destroyed him, in all good ways, often.

He should tell them that. He should tell them that he loved them, again, and that he was sorry a thousand times over. Then he should explain, because he was pretty sure they believed that he was freaking out about the prospect of becoming a father.

And he was. But not like they thought.

He knew it was important that they understand. As soon as possible. But the moment his eyes closed, just to rest them for a second, he dropped into a deep and dreamless sleep.

Chapter Eight

Noel thought he knew his best friend pretty well. He and Jean-Michel had been playing on the same team for a couple years now, had been in Juniors together before that, and been in each other's pockets for most of that time. Anytime the team needed players to share a room, or a ride, or a meal, they did it. And even when the team wasn't putting them together, they spent a lot of time just hanging out, either alone or with their other friends.

And never in all that time had Noel seen Jean-Michel be so quiet.

It was totally freaking Noel out.

He'd tried asking Jean-Michel about it, but he'd just shrugged or waved it away or said nothing.

Jean-Michel had said nothing.

These were not words Noel had ever anticipated might go together. Jean-Michel was what one might call a super-communicator. His style wasn't always effective, or diplomatic, or, hell, even all that sensible, but he *tried* to communicate pretty much all the time.

Noel knew before he did it that he would regret going to Henri with his concerns, so he was unsurprised by Henri's long, sad look expressing all the ways Henri thought Noel was a failure at life. They were huddled together near Henri's car in the airport garage, having just flown in from New York in the middle of the night.

Henri shook his head. "I haven't noticed anything."

"He's worse than Rhian." Actually, Rhian had seemed way better the last couple days, practically smiling all the time on their short road trip.

Henri rolled his eyes. "I don't know what is the matter with either one of them. Maybe you should just ask Jean-Michel yourself."

"I've tried, but he keeps blowing me off."

"When did you ask?" Henri said, like he knew the answer, which was bullshit.

"On the bus to the arena in New York. And before the game. And on the plane on the way home just a little while ago." Noel had acquitted himself well, really.

So he couldn't understand why he was getting the eye-roll again. Honestly, Henri was going to get stuck like that someday.

"Why don't you ask him about it somewhere private?" Henri suggested. "Maybe whatever is bothering him is something he doesn't want to talk about with the team around."

Noel stopped to think about that. It...made sense. Which he sort of hated, but there was a reason he'd come to good old Dad in his hour of need.

"Okay, yeah. That's a good idea. Maybe it will go better if we're alone."

Henri got this strange smile, kind of fond and like he was trying not to roll his eyes again. Weirdo.

Noel thought about it, though, for the ride home and while he was puttering about his apartment the next day. That afternoon at practice Jean-Michel was still mostly silent, almost sullen, so Noel pulled him aside in the locker room.

"How about dinner at your place tonight?"

Jean-Michel blinked up at him, clearly surprised, which Noel didn't get. It wasn't like they didn't do this sort of shit all the time. "Uh, sure."

Noel frowned. "Wait, did you have other plans?"

"No?"

Noel tried not to let his feelings be hurt, but after a couple days of brooding and distance, this reluctance stung.

Noel swallowed all that back and swore to himself he'd get

to the bottom of it tonight. "Okay, so I'll see you in a bit? We can order in, alright?"

"No, I uh—"

Noel was sure he was about to get the brush off.

"I've got salmon," Jean-Michel said, and it took Noel a second to catch up, he'd been so ready to start arguing. Jean-Michel continued, his words picking up speed as he went. "More than enough for two. I bought it—I had you in mind when I bought it. I mean, I thought I would invite you over. So. Yeah. Salmon? Half hour at my place?"

It was Noel's turn to blink in confusion. Finally, he just said, "Yeah, that would be great," as if he'd not invited himself over to begin with.

All the way through the rest of his post-practice routine, including a visit with Savannah to talk about his groin—which wasn't as awkward as it sounded—Noel's mind buzzed with trying to figure out what he could say to convince Jean-Michel to talk to him, and what questions he would ask.

These were totally new concepts for them. Jean-Michel was usually the one trying to get Noel to tell him more. He was the one whose smile lit up a room and set everyone at ease.

By the time Noel showed up at Jean-Michel's door, he was weirdly nervous, but Jean-Michel seemed invested in making their evening as normal as possible. He welcomed Noel with his usual big smile and insult.

"Dude! Come in. If you hang out there, the neighbors will definitely call the cops. Your serial killer haircut makes people nervous, man."

Noel laughed and shook his head. "Shut up." Not everyone could have long, thick hair hanging down to brush their chin and jawline like some people. Noel's fingers itched to touch it, now that his attention was there, but he suppressed his tactile nature, as usual.

"Mario Kart?" Jean-Michel asked while Noel toed off his

shoes and tucked them and his coat in the front hall closet.

"Sure. You need help with dinner?"

"After," Jean-Michel agreed with a shrug. "Beer?"

"Yeah, thanks."

From there, it was a normal night with the two of them. Jean-Michel seemed less reserved than he had in days, and Noel started to relax, laughing when Jean-Michel bumped his shoulder and shoved his arms, trying to force him to crash Princess Peach on her dirt bike, which was never going to happen.

When Noel was finished kicking Jean-Michel's ass, they moved to the kitchen. Noel was pleased to see that Jean-Michel had already set the salmon to marinate, chopped up the broccoli, and measured out the water and rice. It made preparing dinner quick, at least. Noel made Jean-Michel's favorite glaze for the fish, Jean-Michel grilled the salmon perfectly, and they took turns on the rest. They'd done this sort of thing enough to be able to move around the small space between the counters without bumping into each other.

At one point, Jean-Michel slid behind him to get to the sink, his hands resting on Noel's hips for a moment, and Noel's heart sort of sidestepped in his chest.

He took deep breaths until the feeling went away.

They ate in the kitchen, even though their knees tended to bump under this table. Jean-Michel had a nice dining room just around the corner, but they never ate in there.

The conversation started out light enough, and Noel was lulled into a false sense of normalcy until he made the mistake of bringing up how much better Rhian had seemed recently. Jean-Michel went silent again, and stayed that way.

Noel poked at it a little, wondering what the connection was there, but mostly Jean-Michel muttered quick, short answers and changed the subject.

Now Noel was pissed again. He chewed his way through his

dinner and told himself as soon as they were done, he was going to get answers, even if he had to yell. He refused, though, to ruin their meal.

He tried to move the conversation back to the safe topics from before Rhian had come up, but Jean-Michel didn't shake whatever had settled over his mood. By the time they were putting their dishes in the dishwasher, Jean-Michel was practically mute, and Noel was seething.

"Come on, let's go back to the couch," Noel said as soon as they were done, careful to keep his voice even.

Jean-Michel grabbed two beers and followed him, taking his usual place on the couch. At this point, if they'd been about to watch a movie or just chill and talk, Noel would normally take the far end of the sofa, but instead he took what he thought of as his "video game seat" and sat right next to Jean-Michel, turning to pull his leg up on the couch between them, so his knee pressed into Jean-Michel's thigh.

He put a hand on Jean-Michel's bouncing leg to still it and left it there. "Is there something you want to talk about? To tell me?"

Jean-Michel's eyes widened and he swallowed. "What?"

Jesus, he looked *panicked*. "What's going on with you? You've been quiet and acting weird for a couple days. Are you okay?"

Noel watched, confused, as Jean-Michel's shoulders came down from around his ears and the panic left his face.

"Oh, that."

What the fuck else would this have been about? "Yeah, *that.*"

Jean-Michel rubbed his thumb over his lip for a minute, staring at Noel's hand on his knee.

"Are you mad at me? Did I do or say something that upset you?" Noel asked when he couldn't stand it any longer, his stomach squirming with dread.

Jean-Michel's head snapped up. "What? No. No, that's not— shit, I'm sorry. I'm not mad or anything like that. I was just sort of avoiding you."

"Oh, well, that makes me feel much better." Noel pulled his hand back into his lap.

"No! It's not because I *wanted* to avoid you. It's because I wanted to *tell* you."

"Well, that's as clear as mud."

Jean-Michel sighed gustily. "You know what? I'm telling you."

"Telling me what?"

"I went to see Rhian. I went to apologize about being a pain about the woman in the bar that night."

"Okay? I mean, I don't think it was necessary, since he ended up talking to her for an hour, but that's cool."

"Dude, he doesn't live above Savannah's garage."

Noel was having a hard time keeping track of the changes in direction in this conversation. "What? He moved?"

"Not that I know of. He said he lived there three months ago when we were all over there for that barbeque. When would he have had time to secretly move during the season?"

It was a valid point. "Are you sure he doesn't live there?"

"No one lives there. It's completely empty. The door wasn't even locked! I just pushed it open and there was a perfectly empty, kind of crappy, apartment. I don't think he's ever lived there," Jean-Michel added, as though just coming to the realization.

"That's...that's weird," Noel said slowly.

"Right? And also, like, not my business? But it kind of is, because he's my friend and it matters to me that we don't even know where the fuck he lives. And that he's been *lying to us about it.*"

Noel's eyes dropped when Jean-Michel's hand slid over his. Noel didn't remember putting it back on Jean-Michel's knee. He dragged his gaze back up to Jean-Michel's face.

"That's...you're right. That's upsetting. And not okay."

Jean-Michel nodded. He looked sad.

"But you could have told me. Right away, I mean."

"I know. I was being dumb," Jean-Michel admitted with a shrug. "I guess I felt guilty that I'd invited myself over in the first place, so I wasn't even supposed to know. And then when I found out, it was so freaking weird, I didn't know what to do with it."

"I guess I get that," Noel said, letting the relief of having this resolved with Jean-Michel soak in.

"What if he's homeless?" Jean-Michel asked out of nowhere.

"Who? *Rhian?*"

"Yeah."

"He makes, like, *millions of dollars a year*. I seriously doubt he's homeless."

"Okay, then what is it? Is he a spy?"

Noel made a face. "For who? He's American. And didn't he grow up in the foster program in the Midwest somewhere?"

"So? That would be the perfect cover! Drop the kid off and let the government raise him. Like a sleeper cell!"

"And what? Just hope he decides to grow into an agent for a foreign government?"

"Okay, so maybe he's a spy for America. Our jobs do require a lot of travel."

"*To Canada.* I don't think the US government is expending a lot of effort into spying on us. Even you crazy Québécois aren't that scary."

"Hey!" Jean-Michel shouted. "We're very scary."

Noel tried to hide his laughter, but he wasn't doing a very good job of it.

"And, I'd like to point out," Jean-Michel continued, "you are Québécois, too."

"Half," Noel said quickly. He liked to emphasize this to Henri

93

and Jean-Michel every chance he got, because they always got the exact same, identical looks on their faces, just like the one Jean-Michel wore now. Total indignance.

Noel cracked up.

It took him a while to calm down, but he was feeling so relieved, so *happy* to see the smile on Jean-Michel's face, he felt almost drunk with it. When his laughter had finally run its course, he slumped back on the couch and sighed.

"What am I going to do?" Jean-Michel asked quietly.

Noel didn't think before he threw his arm around Jean-Michel's shoulders and pulled him close. "Hey, Hey. What are *we* going to do, okay?"

Jean-Michel practically melted against him, his head on Noel's shoulder. Noel's heart did that funny misstep again, but this time it was a lot harder to breathe through. He got there, though, back to normal except for the scratch in his voice.

"We'll talk to him," he said, making it up as he went along. But really, what other choice did they have? "He's our friend. We'll ask him about it. We'll do what we can to make sure he's okay."

"I don't think he trusts us," Jean-Michel said.

"I don't know," Noel hedged, though part of him agreed, and that sucked. "I mean, maybe I'm a lousy judge of character, but he seems like a good guy. He's been a good friend. I'm sure there's an explanation."

"You think?"

"Yeah. And we'll find out what it is tomorrow."

Rhian stared up at Jean-Michel from his seat on the bench in the locker room. The dude was acting bizarre, and if Rhian didn't know better, he'd ask him if he was on something. His voice had a weird shake to it, and Rhian would swear it was nerves, except he'd seen Jean-Michel face down all manner of vindictive press and whackadoodle fans, and he'd never once heard him sound like this.

He was babbling about the shoot-out drill and then the passing drills, and then Rhian sort of lost the thread. They'd just finished morning skate, and Rhian's focus was more on his hopes to have a few minutes alone with Savannah before he went home to have lunch and a nap with Garrick.

The last few days had been so good. He'd been making an effort to just relax and enjoy their company. He still needed to sit and talk with them, but with the road trip and another game tonight, it hadn't been easy to find a time when they could all talk and not worry that one of them would be dashing off somewhere before they had a chance to settle things.

Jean-Michel finally stopped babbling. After a brief pause, which captured Rhian attention more than the babbling had, he looked Rhian in the eye and said, "Can we talk?"

"Uh, sure? I mean, we are, aren't we?"

Noel chose that moment to slide along the bench until his hip checked Rhian's. He sent Jean-Michel a strange look and just said, "Chill." Then he looked at Rhian. "How about lunch? We can all talk then. It will be more private."

A curl of unease slipped down Rhian's spine, but he shook it off. Maybe the guys had something to tell him.

That thought almost got a smile, because there was always hope these two fucking idiots had finally noticed that each of them was pining for the other.

"Okay. Lunch sounds good," Rhian said, packing away his disappointment at having to miss eating with Garrick. He got to do that all the time, he reminded himself. "Should we maybe go to one of your places, though, if you want privacy?"

"Why don't we go to your place?" Jean-Michel asked. His innocent tone was undermined when a nervous giggle escaped him.

Noel kicked him and turned back to Rhian. "Fucking ignore him. He doubled up at Starbucks this morning."

Rhian's eyes widened. That was just alarming all by itself, but there was something else niggling in the back of his mind. Why had Jean-Michel asked about his place at all? They never went there, obviously.

Before he could sort that out, Henri walked up. "You three okay?" He graced Jean-Michel and his nervous twitching with the same look Rhian was pretty sure he'd been giving him for the past ten minutes.

"Yeah. We're going to lunch. You coming?"

"Sure," Henri answered, his eyes narrowing when Noel opened his mouth as if he might object.

"Great," Noel agreed instead of whatever he was going to say originally. "Let's go back to mine. I'll grab sushi on the way."

Rhian nodded, pleased about the sushi, but also relieved that Dad would be along for this. He had no idea what the fuck was going on with Jean-Michel, or Noel, but he felt like maybe having Dad there to act as a buffer would help if things got weird.

Henri wasn't called Dad for nothing. He was a calming influence on all of them, and if nothing else, Rhian could use a little of that right then.

It wasn't until Rhian was in the car on the way over to Noel's that he started thinking about Jean-Michel asking about going back to his place. The unease came back, tenfold. Rhian, Garrick, and Savannah had been talking, for almost a year now, about actually buying furniture for the in-law apartment above the garage. If nothing else, it would mean they could put up more guests. In fact, that's about all it would mean, because even if Rhian actually had a fake apartment, he would still never invite anyone back to it.

The lies were bad enough already. That would be another level he couldn't stand.

When he got to Noel's, he parked right behind Henri and followed him into the building and up to Noel's place. Noel and Jean-Michel were already there, spreading out the frankly ludicrous amount of sushi on the kitchen's long breakfast bar.

It was a little early for lunch, but they'd had practice, so they all dug into the mountain of food in front of them, any conversation temporarily stalled in favor of stuffing their faces.

Rhian was happily eating his spicy tuna roll and sharing looks with Henri about the idiots across the breakfast bar, when Jean-Michel suddenly put down his chopsticks and caught Rhian's gaze.

"Why is your apartment empty?"

Rhian paused with his chopsticks halfway to his mouth. "What?"

Henri cocked his head curiously, looking between Jean-Michel and Rhian.

Jean-Michel had the grace to look guilty, but he held Rhian's gaze. "I stopped by your apartment the other day, because I felt bad about the bar and making you go talk with that woman when you clearly didn't want to. The door was unlocked. I didn't mean to put my nose in where it doesn't belong, but it's kind of weird, dude. Your apartment is empty."

Ryan stood from his stool, his heart pounding against his ribs. The sushi was dangerously close to making a reappearance. "I'm staying with a friend."

"And you took all your furniture?" Noel asked.

Rhian could tell they were trying hard not to sound accusatory. Or judgmental. Or any of the zillion different ways they could reasonably sound, given than they'd figured out that their supposed good friend had been lying to them. For years.

"I'm going to go," he managed, turning for the door. He wished his voice had sounded steadier, but it probably didn't make much difference at this point.

He heard Jean-Michel's quiet, "What the fuck?", and Noel's

even softer, "Woah," but he didn't stop moving.

He slid his sneakers on, left them untied. Didn't bother pulling on his coat before yanking open the door. He was almost into the hallway, almost free, when a hand landed on his shoulder.

He froze. Didn't look back.

"Are you okay to drive?" Henri asked quietly.

Rhian nodded, his eyes filling with tears at *this*, of all things. Fucking Dad.

Henri let him go. Rhian ran from the building.

Garrick was pulling the ingredients for his lunch and Rhian's afternoon snack from the fridge when the back door flew open so fast, the Christmas wreath fell from the door and landed on the mudroom floor with a thud.

Garrick watched, slack-jawed, as Rhian stomped in, slapped it back up on its hook, and shut the door hard enough that it was a miracle the damn thing didn't fall off again.

"What—"

The question died when Rhian's head snapped up, his eyes wet and red.

Garrick's heart broke a little, and he didn't even know what had happened yet. He came around the kitchen island toward Rhian, every instinct on high alert. Had Rhian had a panic attack? Had something happened?

He put his hands up, to hold Rhian. To anchor him.

He was brought up short, though, when Rhian pushed him back and walked right past.

"Rhi?" Garrick asked, uncertain and hurt.

Rhian just shook his head, his feet moving faster and faster away from Garrick until he was sprinting up the stairs.

Alone.

Garrick didn't understand. Rhian would come to them when he was feeling alone. Lost. Scared. Anything. That was what they did for him. That was what they did for one another.

Except, apparently, not this time. Not for the past few weeks.

Garrick stood there, dumbfounded, for a long minute. Then he dug his phone out of his pocket and called Savannah.

As soon as she answered, he said, "You need to come home."

Chapter Nine

Savannah hovered in the doorway to their bedroom, watching Rhian. He lay flat on his back on the bed, his eyes glued to the ceiling.

She would have thought he was getting ready to take his pre-game nap a little early, if it weren't for the fact that he was fully clothed on top of the covers, and the set of his shoulders was far too tight for anyone who was hoping to sleep.

He also kept taking deep, shaky breaths and letting them out slowly.

Part of Savannah—the chicken-shit part that she would ignore—wanted to just leave him be. Let him rest and recover from whatever the hell had happened at lunch. It had taken more willpower than she would have thought she possessed not to call the French Canadian Mafia as she was tearing home from the rink. If she found out they'd done something shitty, she was going to be hard pressed not to subject them to a "tape-to-thigh waxing" when she was prepping them for tonight's game.

There was nothing like having all those little hairs ripped out to make a man reconsider his sad choices.

That would have to wait, though, until she had a better idea of what was going on. It was Savannah's habit to stay in the office until she had to move to the big rink for the game, so she only had about two hours before her absence would not just be noted, but a problem.

She entered the bedroom and walked around to the side of the bed. Rhian barely moved, only his eyes tracking her movement.

"Hey, you okay?" she asked, which seemed like a foolish question but she had to start somewhere.

Rhian frowned. "I'm fine."

"You very clearly are not fine," Savannah said. She ran her fingers through Rhian's soft blond curls, as was her habit.

Rhian sighed and closed his eyes. "It's fine. I'll be fine."

"Can we please talk about it?" she asked. She'd beg if she had to. "We'd like to know what's going on. What's got you so upset."

Movement caught her eye and she saw Garrick in the door, watching them. He'd taken an extra minute to settle himself before coming upstairs. Rhian rebuffing him earlier was not something he took lightly, and he was hurt.

"There's nothing to talk about," Rhian said abruptly, waving his hand in front of himself and right at her belly. "I can't change it now."

Savannah took a quick step back, pressing her palm protectively over her stomach. "What?"

Rhian sat bolt upright in bed. "No!" He stood so quickly she took another step back. "That's not—my god, no, that's not what I meant at all."

Rhian pulled her against his chest and hung on. She clung back, trying to get her heart to beat normally again, to make her breathing calm. Garrick wrapped them both in his arms.

"I think you better tell us what's going on, Rhian," Garrick said firmly. "We need to stop these misunderstandings before they start to leave permanent damage."

Rhian went rigid between them. "God, has it been that bad?"

Savannah ran a soothing hand down his back but was still brutally honest. "I get that you're having a hard time accepting this baby, Rhian."

Rhian jerked upright, separating himself from them both. "No, I'm not!"

The three of them stood looking at each other for a moment.

Finally, Garrick ventured, "You're not?"

"No! Is that—" Rhian swallowed heavily. "Is that what you thought?"

"What else were we supposed to think?" Savannah asked, careful to keep her tone level. "You were so happy when we found out, but then you never talked about it. Until this week, you never even touched my belly or anything."

"That was just...you didn't want us to touch your breasts. I wasn't sure what would bother you and what wouldn't. And I didn't mean to not touch you. I mean, I did touch you. We had sex and stuff, still. We touch a lot, don't we?" he asked, and he didn't sound sure, like maybe what he thought was a lot wasn't to Savannah.

Savannah stepped closer and threaded their fingers together. "Yes, we do."

Rhian nodded. "Okay, good. Right."

"But if it's not the baby," she continued doggedly, "what has been eating at you?"

Garrick's fingers tangled with Rhian's other hand and squeezed.

"It's the baby," Rhian said, "but not the way you think." He looked at Savannah. "I want this baby so much. I want you both so much, and I want to have a huge family with you, and I can't *wait* to see what he or she looks like and spoil them at Christmas and all the rest, it's just..."

They waited, and when it was clear Rhian was trying to find the words and failing, Garrick pulled them over to the bed and sat, tugging Rhian down beside him. Savannah stood between Rhian's legs and ran her hand over his head, his shoulder. Garrick pulled him close with one arm and held Savannah's hand with the other.

They waited.

"I'm worried the baby won't really be mine," he said at last.

Savannah sucked in a breath and caught Garrick's wide, stricken eyes.

"What do you mean?" Garrick asked carefully. Savannah

worried that she knew, but appreciated that Garrick wasn't jumping to conclusions as quickly. "I thought we'd already talked about this. We said it didn't matter whose DNA actually got the job done."

"Yeah, no. Hell, I hope he or she looks like you," he said with a small smile for Garrick.

"Me? Why?"

"You're the most beautiful man in the world, to me. Of course I want our children to look like the people I love most already."

Garrick looked stunned.

Savannah rubbed her hand over Rhian's shoulder. "So, I guess we don't understand. What do you mean, the baby won't really be yours?"

Rhian looked up at her and she watched his eyes fill with tears. It felt like a steel band was cinching around her chest.

"Because no one can know. And I get why, I know that this baby, and any others we have, will have to be seen by the world as yours and Garrick's. I get that it's important that no one at work know about us. I can't...I can't be the one to bring my baby to the holiday party or family skate. That your job depends on it. I understand all the reasons, but all I can think about is what it means, you know? It means that there will be times they shouldn't call me Dad. Or Poppa." Rhian's voice cracked hard on *poppa* and he swallowed hard. "We'll have to raise our children to know that I'm one name at home and another everywhere else. How can we ask a little baby to do that? I don't want them to have to lie. The way I always, always have to lie."

Savannah wiped at the tears streaming down her face. She was ashamed of herself for thinking Rhian didn't want the baby. Or that he was afraid of becoming a parent and that was what was freaking him out so bad. She should have known that all he was thinking about *was* the baby, and how to be the best parent he possibly could.

"Do you know why I like Christmas so much?" Rhian asked, out of nowhere.

Savannah thought about the answer and realized she didn't. She could tell from Garrick's expression that he didn't either. In fact, now that she thought about it, she was pretty sure Rhian had hated it until the last few years.

"It's because of our families. Christmas is the one time of year I'm sure we're going to see a ton of family. Mine, both of yours. And they all know. They know the truth, and while it still weirds some of them out," he added, jostling Garrick with his elbow, "we can be ourselves. We don't have to pretend. I can be in love with both of you, and you can be in love with me, and it's not just when we're alone in this house."

Savannah felt like someone had just kicked her in the chest.

"I'm so sorry," she said, not sure which of the many things she owed him an apology for she was trying to cover.

"It's not your fault. Not any more than it's any of our faults. It's just...the way it is. And I've been trying, for a while now, to wrap my head around it. The fact that this is the way it has to be, but it's kind of killing me, too, you know? I love you. I love your families, and my family, and *our* family—which is not something I thought I would ever be able to say—and I can't acknowledge any of them, let alone tell everyone how fucking awesome it is to love and be loved by these amazing people."

Savannah smiled through her tears, because it *was* fucking awesome.

"So, that's what's been eating at me, I guess," Rhian said, his voice hoarse and low. "And I'm trying to get through it, to accept what needs to be accepted, but it's fucking hard."

Garrick shook his head, like maybe he couldn't accept it either. "Yeah. This is...this is a lot."

"It is," Rhian said grimly. "It's really a lot. And then at lunch today Jean-Michel asked me why my apartment was empty,

104

because he apparently stopped by the other day. And I forced out another lie, but it was weak, and then I ran."

Savannah's heart lurched and she traded a quick look with Garrick.

"And Seamus basically insisted that I invite the guys to his holiday party, but that means more lies, you know? Now I can't just tuck myself in a corner surrounded by our family and be myself and be *honest*. Instead, I have to hang out with friends who think I'm some kind of fucking homeless orphan or something, and pretend Seamus is just my friend, and Chelsea is his granddaughter, not my sister. With the guys there, I'll have to avoid her or they'll think I'm hitting on her. You know that, right? People already think that and it makes me sick, but if it's just strangers, who cares? But I can't deal with that from the guys. I can't. And I can't tell them the truth."

"Why can't you?" Savannah asked.

"About Seamus? About my family? You know Seamus doesn't want that. If it got out, he'd have to acknowledge that his daughter...that his daughter, my biological mother, abandoned a baby. The whole sordid story would come out, and then maybe that guy who Chelsea thinks is my dad will figure shit out, and the press, and..."

"Do you really care about all that?" Garrick asked.

"I don't, but I know Seamus does."

"How would you feel if Seamus did acknowledge you? If you could call him Grandfather in public? I had sort of thought you weren't interested in that getting out, either."

"No, you're right. I didn't want to tell people. Not at first. But I've been thinking about it a lot recently, and realized now I wouldn't mind." Rhian smiled, such a sad wistful twist of lips that Savannah felt more tears stinging her already aching eyes. "Actually, I think it would be cool," Rhian added quietly, "to be able to call them family in public. To invite Seamus to the fathers' events with the team and stuff."

Savannah exchanged a look with Garrick—one that promised another conversation later. One where they could both berate themselves for so thoroughly missing something so massively important.

The Seamus thing, though, wasn't up to them to fix. But there was another part of this they could help with. And Savannah knew that was really all down to her.

"What about the guys?" she asked, glancing at Garrick to see his eyebrows go up. She nodded to tell him she was sure.

Well, she was mostly sure.

Fuck, this was going to be a huge risk. But when she looked back at Rhian, it felt worth it. Terrifying, but worth it.

"What about the guys?" Rhian asked back.

"You could tell them the truth."

"About Seamus and Chelsea?"

"No. Well, yes. I think they would keep it to themselves. But also about us."

Rhian's mouth dropped open. He sat staring up at her blankly.

It took a long, long time for him to close his mouth, and even then, all he managed to say was, "What?"

Garrick looked between Rhian and Savannah. It felt like they were teetering on the edge of a cliff. A cliff that apparently they'd been crawling steadily towards for years, but had accelerated to an all-out run with this pregnancy.

In hindsight, it had been really fucking stupid of all three of them not to figure out this would happen.

He watched them closely, trying to gauge how freaked out Savannah was about making this offer, and how likely Rhian was to accept it. Garrick, for his part, didn't know *what* to think.

The truth was, Savannah was the only female head trainer in

106

the entire league. In almost any men's professional league, for that matter, in any sport. She'd been doing nothing but sterling work since coming to Boston, and her reputation among players and management was as a hard-ass workaholic. More importantly, though, the *players* trusted her. More than the doctors, management, their agents. The players came to her, mostly about stuff to do with training but sometimes with other stuff, to talk shit out with her before they made a move.

She was already worried about how management was going to deal with the pregnancy, since it was an issue they were almost entirely unfamiliar with outside the administrative side of the business. The whole world finding out that Savannah was in love and having a baby with two men, one of whom was *a player on her team*, would be a disaster. At best, management would make her life miserable until she quit. At worst, she could be harassed by players, management, and the press alike, or fired, and Rhian could get traded to the other side of the continent.

Now, she wasn't talking about telling the whole world. But she was talking about telling three people who were not only not members of this family, but were also teammates of Rhian's, and Savannah's responsibility in many ways.

"We can't," Rhian said at last, and Garrick tried hard not to feel relief.

"We could," Savannah offered with remarkable speed.

"No." Rhian shook his head. "They're not just my friends, they're both of our coworkers. I can't put you at risk like that."

"I'm putting me at risk like that. I'm saying you should do it."

Rhian looked to Garrick for help, but he was staying out of this. His job was clear—support them both, no matter how this shook out. He could give advice, but they both knew their own minds, and the personalities involved, far better than he, and it wasn't his career on the line. He was the perfectly happy part owner of a minor league hockey team in Canada, and since one of the other owners, Savannah's brother Callum, had married

Rupert, the team's manager, in one of the most public and widely reported weddings in the past year, it wasn't like the world finding out about Garrick was going to blow the doors off the arena.

Which didn't mean Garrick wasn't terrified, of course, but he also understood, after hearing what Rhian had told them, why it was worth the risk. It was absolutely worth the risk...if Savannah was okay with it.

Rhian took both of Savannah's hands in his. "Do you really trust them that much?"

"Yes," she said, but Garrick had caught the hesitation.

So had Rhian. "You don't."

"No, I do. It's just..." Savannah frowned and looked up at the ceiling for a second. "Okay, how about this? I absolutely trust Henri. No questions, no doubts. In fact, I'm pretty sure he's known for weeks that I'm pregnant and he hasn't said a word to me or anyone else. So, what if you start there?"

"He's married," Garrick pointed out. "Do we trust his wife? Because it's not fair to tell him something he can't tell her."

"Yeah, Lisa is cool," Savannah said with a nod. "She's been dragged through this league for years and I've never heard her say a word about anyone or anything, not even when we had both had a couple too many at last year's holiday party. She's probably got shit locked in her vault that would shock us all."

"What a terrifying thought," Rhian said.

"So, we agree? Henri? As a start?" Savannah said.

Rhian studied Savannah's face, every shift of expression, for a long time. When he couldn't detect anything but sincerity, even if there was a tinge of nerves, he looked to Garrick, who nodded encouragingly.

"Okay," Rhian said, his heart beating hard. "I'd like to do it here, if that's okay with you guys. I'd like you to be with me."

"Sure," Garrick said easily. "I know we were going to spend tomorrow morning being slobs around the house, but how about we have Henri over for breakfast? I don't think we should drag this out."

"Yeah, that's a good idea," Savannah said. "Band-Aid approach is good."

Rhian frowned at the analogy, but he couldn't find fault with it. This was going to be riding him, a constant itch under his skin until it was done and he was sure they weren't making a catastrophic mistake.

Though, while he was nervous about telling Henri, but he wasn't too worried about Henri telling anyone else. He was more worried about Henri's reaction. About Henri thinking it was weird or wrong.

Rhian would hate to lose that friendship.

He must have been sitting there, staring into space for too long, because Savannah patted his shoulder and pushed him back on the bed.

"Come on. Time for pre-game naps."

"Naps? Plural?" Rhian asked.

"Hell, yes," Garrick agreed, shucking his jeans before going to work on Rhian's and then tossing them over the footboard. "That was fucking exhausting."

"You're telling me," Savannah said as she set the alarm on her phone and set it down on the bedside table. As soon as she'd tossed off her jeans and fleece, Rhian dragged her across the bed until she was pressed to his chest.

Garrick curled around her back and threw his arm over both of them.

Rhian was still telling them both how much he loved them when he fell asleep.

He woke briefly when Savannah's alarm went off an hour

later, but she told him to go back to sleep, and he did, until Garrick woke him an hour after that.

He and Garrick had a nice pregame snack tucked close together in the breakfast nook, not really saying much. Then Rhian loaded up his gear and headed out the door. He saw one of his spare jerseys hanging in the mudroom and asked Garrick about it.

"I'm going to go to the game tonight."

"Yeah?" Garrick went to a bunch of games every year, but usually they were special occasion kind of games, with an award being handed out or something. "Any reason?"

"I just want to be close to you, I guess."
Rhian smiled and made sure Garrick knew what he thought of that with a long, sweet kiss.

Chapter Ten

On the face of things, Henri had received far stranger and more worrisome summons than the one to breakfast with Rhian this morning, but he also suspected that there were surprises in store for him yet.

The first came when Savannah opened the door in old yoga pants and a long-sleeve t-shirt with Rhian's name and number on it. That was...interesting. And Henri couldn't help but wonder if that was supposed to be a hint, or if Savannah was just showing her support for Rhian.

Garrick came out of the kitchen wearing a *Give Blood, Play Hockey* apron in brilliant red, a spatula in one hand and a tea towel in the other.

"Henri," Garrick said with an easy grin. "Can I get you a coffee? Tea? Juice?"

Henri smiled, always pleased to hear his name pronounced correctly south of the border. "Coffee and water, if it's not too much trouble. I could also get it myself, if you point me in the right direction."

"Nah, you go on through to the dining room," Garrick said, waving the way with his spatula. "We'll be right in."

Henri turned just in time to see Rhian vault down the last few stairs of the main staircase in the front hall. He'd apparently been upstairs. In his socks. And a ratty pair of jeans and a t-shirt.

Henri thought about that for a moment, then turned back and looked at Garrick. Garrick just raised his eyebrows, as if daring Henri to ask the question.

Henri demurred, for now, and moved toward the dining room. He was pretty sure, though, that he had an idea of what was going on. When he found himself sitting across the table from Savannah, who was slowly sipping her tea and nibbling on plain toast, Henri thought about asking her if she liked being a beard for the gay couple living in this house with her. Then he recalled the reason she might need to start the day with such a bland breakfast, and he got confused again.

Surrogate? Or maybe he was wrong, and she wasn't pregnant.

Once Garrick and Rhian had carried in a huge breakfast of eggs, bacon, french toast, fresh fruit and juice, and Savannah had plowed through a really impressive portion of it, he knew he was right about one thing.

There was no *way* that lady wasn't pregnant.

The rest, though, was still a mystery. They ate, chatting companionably, and Henri was pleased to confirm that he enjoyed Savannah's company as much or more outside the office, and that Garrick was a great guy. It even turned out that Garrick knew one of Henri's friends from playing for McGill. It was easy, comfortable, and confusing as hell since Henri knew the reason he'd been asked over today was not to prove that Garrick was a wonderful cook or that Savannah could eat half a loaf of french toast.

Whatever it was Rhian wanted to tell him was obviously still on Rhian's mind, though he made no indication he was ready to say anything. He did, however, become increasingly quiet as the last of the food disappeared from their plates.

Henri broke first.

"Come on, kid. You can tell me anything. I'm not going to judge you."

Rhian stared at him, blank faced, as if this wasn't the reason Henri was here in the first place.

Henri backpedaled. "Or not. It's okay, either way."

"No, I want to tell you something," Rhian said suddenly.

Henri sat back and waited.

"I'm in love with, and in a relationship with, both Garrick and Savannah, and I live here with them, so that's why the apartment is empty."

For a long moment, Henri just digested that, because he'd thought he was pretty clever and had figured some shit out, but he hadn't seen that one coming at all. Damn it, he was sort of disappointed in himself. Because now that he thought about it, it made perfect sense.

He finally spoke when it looked as though Rhian was going to expire from nerves, and Garrick and Savannah were both staring at him as if they could will him, with the power of their minds alone, to be decent about this.

There wasn't any need for that, of course.

Henri smiled, pitying the terror on Rhian's face. "Relax, Rhian. It's cool. Good for you—all three of you." He nodded to Savannah and Garrick, who positively beamed back at him.

"Yeah?" Rhian said, still uncertain.

"Yeah, kid. Come on. What kind of asshole do you think I am?"

"No, I don't—I wouldn't have told you if I thought that."

Holy shit, the kid was still wound tight about it, though. "I get it. This can't be easy to keep under wraps."

Rhian shrugged, and his lovers frowned. "Only family knows, really. A few close friends," Rhian admitted.

That sounded rough, but Henri was also flattered. "Thank you for trusting me, then," he said. He made sure they understood he speaking to all three of them. "Are you going to tell anyone else?"

Rhian caught his eyes and Henri knew they were thinking about the same two idiots. Rhian looked so painfully uncertain.

Henri sighed. "Are you worried they'll judge you or some shit, or are you worried they'll tell someone they shouldn't?"

Rhian shrugged. "Maybe a little of the first, and a bit more of the second."

"The first is bullshit," Henri said firmly. "I mean really, they have no room to judge, since it's blatantly obvious to everyone but the two of them that they're pining for each other."

Garrick snorted. "How does someone not know they are pining for someone?"

"I don't know, but those two are totally pulling it off," Savannah confirmed.

Henri laughed, delighted to know that he and Rhian weren't the only ones suffering.

"And the second thing?" Rhian asked, worrying his lower lip with his teeth.

"Tell them they can't tell anyone and they won't. You know they won't."

Rhian sat and thought about that. Henri turned to Savannah. "What do you think?"

"About telling Noel and Jean-Michel? I feel better knowing you trust them with it."

"Good. Because let's be real—if they tell anyone, it's your ass as much or more than Rhian's." Savannah nodded. She looked grateful that he'd understood that. He turned back to Rhian. "Tell the boys that. Remind them it's not just about you. They'll get it. They won't do anything to hurt Savannah."

"They won't?" Garrick asked curiously.

"Nah. They love her."

A twinkle entered Garrick's eyes. "Do they, now?"

Savannah rolled her eyes. "Not like that, you idiot. And god help me if they did. Like I don't have my hands full with the two of you."

"She's right. It's not that kind of love," Henri reassured Garrick. "They think of her as sort of the team mom."

"They *what?*" Savannah asked, outraged.

"Haven't you ever noticed they're always coming to you for advice? Or sitting around your office making a nuisance of

114

themselves when they've had a hard loss?"

"Well, yes," Savannah said slowly. "But I just thought they needed their trainer."

"Do you think the trainer out in LA helps the boys choose their Christmas gifts for their wives and mothers?"

"Well—but—"

"Or maybe the guy in New York has spent a two-hour long flight quizzing the rookie from Quebec City on English verb conjugation?" Henri laughed at the resignation settling over Savannah. "They spend more time with you in your room or office than they do in the locker room," he told her.

Savannah's shoulders slumped. "I thought they'd just sort of followed Rhian."

Rhian bit his lip, but failed to stifle his laughter. "Actually, most of the time, I was just following *them*."

"Oh, my god." Savannah pointed an accusatory finger at Rhian. "You knew! Why didn't you ever say anything?"

"What? That two of my closest friends think of my girlfriend like a surrogate mother?"

"Yes!" Savannah said, indignant.

"Are you kidding? I never said anything because I wanted to get laid again. Like, ever."

Garrick laughed, loud and bright. Savannah rolled her eyes, but grudgingly nodded as if to say Rhian had a fair point.

Henri grinned, pleased to have material to tease Savannah with, who he was feeling much closer to than he had in all the time they'd been working together. He'd always assumed she held herself a little apart from the rest of the team outside of work hours because it was the safest route to protect her professional reputation, but now he knew it was even more complicated than that.

He was happy to have been allowed through at least some of those carefully constructed walls.

115

These three were a nice...well, not a couple. Thruple? Threesome? Whatever. They made a nice relationship unit, and he'd be happy to spend time with them outside of work.

Savannah walked Henri to the door, smiling as he chirped the boys for their "disgustingly domestic display" while they bickered over who should do the dishes. They were both claiming they should be the one, which was the opposite of what most people had to deal with. Savannah was pretty sure some of her girlfriends would kill for this problem.

"You have a nice family here," Henri said when they reached the foyer and relative quiet.

"Thank you."

She was surprised when Henri leaned in and kissed each of her cheeks once. When he stepped back, he said, "I hope that's okay. I figure we aren't just coworkers anymore, what with me knowing all your secrets."

"Well, not *all* of them," she said with a sly smile and a waggle of her eyebrows.

Henri threw back his head and hooted with laughter.

She recognized that this wasn't something she would ever have dared say to or in front of the guys at work—to Henri's point. Having a woman traveling with the team, one who was constantly in and out of the locker room, climbing all over them in her office, yelling at them in the gym, and on the bench for games, meant that it was easiest if she didn't ever let them see her flirt or dole out an innuendo, let alone laugh about or talk about anything sexual.

It meant, though, that most of her colleagues had little to no idea who she really was. It was nice, now, to have an exception. She was getting a small taste of what Rhian must have been feeling and felt both guilty for not having realized, and relieved to have someone like Henri in both of their lives.

116

Rhian was right. This was definitely better.

Still, there had to be rules.

"No kissing at the office," Savannah said mock-sternly as she helped Henri with his coat.

"I would never," Henri said, far more seriously. "I don't know how you put up with the shit you do already. I can promise you, I will never do anything that would make that worse for you."

"Thanks," Savannah said. "I have to be honest, I didn't think anyone but Rhian really saw it."

"I see it. I've seen it. I've even thought about offering my help if you needed it, but I suspected that might land me a nice bald patch on my thigh."

Savannah's cheeks warmed. "I have no idea what you're talking about," she said as innocently as she could manage.

Henri chuckled. "You do what you have to. Though, now that I've mentioned the offer, you should know it stands. If there is ever anything I can do for you, or for you and Rhian, you just let me know."

"Thanks, Henri," Savannah said, her mind already working on a few ideas. "I may take you up on that."

She waited at the door until Henri was in his car, then waved as he pulled away from the curb.

Smiling, she went back toward the kitchen, wondering why the arguing had stopped and the water wasn't running. She found her boys standing in the middle of the kitchen, kissing.

"And people wonder why I worry about leaving you alone. The dishes will never get done," she said teasingly.

Rhian grinned at her over his shoulder. "Sorry. We were celebrating." He reached out for her hand and she took his.

"I think that went well," she said.

Rhian tugged her closer, then sat in one of the kitchen chairs. She didn't fight it when he drew her onto his lap. "It did."

"Feeling any better?"

"I am," Rhian said, shifting her in his lap a little so she could feel how much better.

"Honestly, you two," she admonished, even as she could feel her pulse speeding up a little. "Henri was right in the front hall!"

"He was leaving," Garrick said as he pulled up a chair and sat close.

"Thank god he didn't forget anything," she chided, but she was laughing. "It's one thing to know, it's another thing to see it."

"I think Henri would be just fine," Rhian said, his hand skating up her thigh. "I totally caught him checking out Garrick's ass when he went to get the fresh coffee."

"He did not!" Garrick said.

Rhian grinned. "He did."

Savannah was distracted by their teasing, so she was startled by the drag of Rhian's fingers along the elastic of her underwear.

"You know what I was thinking?" Savannah asked, quickly getting into the spirit of things, so to speak.

"That, statistically speaking, Rhian has probably managed to befriend all the gay or bi guys on the team?" Garrick asked.

"Well, yes, that," she agreed, while Rhian huffed and rolled his eyes.

"And?" Garrick prompted.

"And," she agreed, "when Noel, Jean-Michel, and Henri all know, maybe we can ask them to run interference for us when we're on road trips. They can be your alibi or whatever so you can spend more nights in my room."

Rhian's fingers paused as they snuck beneath the waistband of her sweats. "Yeah?"

God, she liked the smile in his eyes. The hope radiating from them. "Yeah. I mean, only if you want to."

Rhian tugged her down for a long kiss that was still almost

118

chaste as he thanked her or agreed with her or whatever the hell he was trying to convey.

At this point, she was really distracted by his hand in her pants. Goddamn, pregnancy hormones were a thing of wonder.

She only whimpered a little when Rhian pulled away. "So, this means you're okay with telling the guys?"

"If you and Henri both trust them, then yes."

Rhian pulled her in again, holding her tight against his chest. She hugged him back. Garrick ran his hands over them both, staying close.

"Thank you," Rhian said.

"Does it help?"

"Yes. It does," he said quickly, sincerely. "I'm not interested in having a lot of people speculate about my private life. You know that. And I can't tell them about my bio family, no matter how much I love them. So, I just needed...I just needed some more of the people I care about to know at least some of the truth about me, I guess."

"And we can tell other people, eventually," Garrick said gently. "We can talk about it, and we'll decide as we go, right?" She and Rhian nodded. It was still terrifying, but it also still felt like it was the right thing to do. It still felt worth it.

Chapter Eleven

Garrick hovered behind Rhian, who hovered behind the goddamn butler Seamus had hired for his holiday party, who hovered by the door, waiting for guests to arrive. There were already easily seventy people in the house, including a large number of people who counted as their family, but Rhian was determined to snag his friends the minute they walked through the door.

Henri and Lisa had the dubious honor of arriving first. Before they could even get to Rhian and Garrick, the children were invited to the party being held for them downstairs, and were then whisked away by one of the horde of caretakers and entertainers Seamus had hired.

Lisa waved goodbye, delighted, then greeted Rhian and Garrick with a big smile, shrugging off her wrap into the waiting arms of her husband, who passed it and his coat to the butler with a bemused expression. Lisa then kissed them on both cheeks and stood back so her husband could do the same.

Henri then assessed the looks on both their faces and burst out laughing.

"I don't know that you expected when you set yourselves up at the welcoming committee."

"I'm actually waiting for Jean-Michel and Noel, not you, old man."

"He's determined to tell them this evening," Garrick added. He figured it wouldn't hurt to have Henri aware of what was happening.

"Excellent," Henri said cheerfully. "I love a good ambush."

Rhian frowned, but the minute the doorbell rang again, he turned away to see who was coming through the door.

Lisa rolled her eyes. "On that note, I see a very handsome

bartender who looks like he wants to be my friend."

Henri patted Garrick's shoulder sympathetically. "Grab me before you go wherever you're going to drag them off to, and I'll come along."

Garrick studied his face. "Are you worried?"

"Not really," Henri said with an easy shrug. "But I can't pass up an excuse to smack them if they do anything other than smile immediately."

Garrick grinned. "Fair enough." He appreciated Henri's protectiveness. It was, after all, why Garrick hadn't left Rhian's side. He had every intention of being there when he told his friends, just in case it didn't go down as planned.

Noel and Jean-Michel finally arrived twenty minutes later, together, and without dates. As Garrick understood it, this had come to be expected.

He'd met them a few times before, but hadn't really gotten to know them as well as he'd wished. He was hoping that after tonight, he wouldn't have to force that reticence and they could all hang out some. What he did know of them, through Rhian, was enough to think they'd get along great.

He greeted them both in French—he'd gone to university in Montreal, after all—and their eyes widened. He figured they were wildly impressed until Jean-Michel said, "Good god, you're from the Maritimes, aren't you?"

Yeah, Garrick thought to himself, he was going to like them just fine.

He led the way to the bar, Jean-Michel and Noel teasing Rhian the whole way about his fancy friends. If either of them noticed that Rhian was being quieter than usual, they didn't call him out on it. Garrick did catch them exchanging a long look, though.

He also noted the way their shoulders brushed, and that their eyes only very rarely strayed from one another. They weren't rude, but they were very, transparently, aware of each other.

While they ordered their drinks, Garrick sidled over to Henri. "Can you get away for a moment?" Garrick tried not to be too obvious while he watched Lisa flirting with the handsome bartender.

The man was definitely interested.

Henri rolled his eyes. "You know, I have you to blame for this," he said in French, gesturing at his wife's back.

Garrick responded in kind. "Pardon?"

"She's decided we should reassess our life goals, now that she's heard about you three."

Garrick swallowed his drink wrong and started coughing.

"She seems to think," Henri continued, as if Garrick wasn't turning blue right beside him, "that we should—and I quote— explore our options."

Garrick blinked back the tears in his eyes and took a healthy slug of his drink, this time successfully navigating it to his stomach instead of his lungs.

"You're welcome?" he offered.

"Well, someday I'll either thank you or punch you in the face, I suspect."

"I respect that."

Henri looked over his wife's shoulder at the man smiling down at her, and rolled his eyes. "She's barking up the wrong tree, of course. Again. She's terrible at guessing."

"You don't think he's interested? He looks interested," Garrick said, hoping he wasn't accelerating the timeline on getting punched.

"Oh, he's practically panting for her, but he hasn't cast me so much as a glance."

Garrick looked at Henri and smiled. "Ah."

Henri took a sip of his drink. "Indeed. Not something I ever really gave a lot of thought, but I'm too old to pretend it was just because he and I were roommates in juniors, don't you think?"

Garrick wasn't sure what to say to that, but was saved from trying when Rhian nudged his side. "Let's go to the study."

"Yes," Henri said briskly, "lets."

Rhian led the way down the main hallway and on to the back of the house, holding the door open into the small, cozy room where Seamus did most of his work. As they all filed in, Noel remarked, "You really know your way around this place. Will Mr. Lynch mind that we're back here?"

While Rhian shrugged that off, Garrick subtly turned face down the picture on the desk of Rhian and his sister Chelsea. It wasn't, in fact, a room that guests were welcome to use. But then, Rhian wasn't a guest, and this wasn't even the first time Garrick had been dragged in here for a private conversation tonight. He hoped this one went as well as the one he had with Seamus earlier.

"I have something to tell you both," Rhian said instead of explaining anything at all about Seamus, and Garrick got a glimpse at how good he'd gotten at avoiding lying when he could. It made him sad, and all the more resolved that this was the right thing to do.

Noel immediately turned to Henri. "And he's not telling you?"

"I know already," Henri said mildly.

Jean-Michel huffed indignantly. "Why does he get to know first?"

"*Not important,*" Rhian said long-sufferingly.

Noel seemed to get that what Rhian did have to say *was* important, so when Jean-Michel opened his mouth to say something else, Noel silenced him by grabbing his wrist and squeezing.

"What's up?" Noel said. He seemed calm and receptive.

"I want to explain my apartment and a few other things, but what I'm going to tell you is not something you can ever share with anyone else. Ever. Is that cool?"

Noel nodded immediately. Jean-Michel shrugged.

Henri knocked him in the back of the head.

"Yeah, it's cool. I swear. You want to do pinky promises or something?" Jean-Michel said.

Rhian looked for a moment as if he was questioning all his life choices.

"Go on, Rhi. You can trust us," said Noel, and that seemed to settle something for both Rhian and Jean-Michel. Garrick definitely liked Noel, at least.

"I'm in a relationship with Savannah."

"I knew it!" Jean-Michel crowed.

"And Garrick."

Jean-Michel's mouth snapped shut. He turned to look at Garrick, then back at Rhian. "What?"

"We three," Rhian continued determinedly, "are in one relationship together. We're in love."

"Huh," Noel said, then he lifted his fist. When Rhian bumped it, albeit hesitantly, Noel smiled. "Nice."

"I don't get it," Jean-Michel said.

Henri looked at the ceiling as if it might grant him patience before turning to Jean-Michel. "What part don't you get?"

"Do the three of you...I mean, all at the same time, like..."

Rhian's cheeks turned pink and Garrick thought he looked fucking adorable. He took mercy and went to put an arm around Rhian's shoulders. "We all share one bedroom, with one bed in it. Does that answer your question?"

Jean-Michel's eyes widened in what could only be described as awe. He gave Garrick a once-over that made Garrick blush and

Henri laugh.

"Dude, you are one lucky sonofabitch!" Jean-Michel announced.

Garrick supposed he'd take it as a compliment, anyway.

"And I'm *so glad* you're not a spy," Jean-Michel continued.

"Oh my god," Henri muttered.

Seamus circulated through his house, greeting guests and catching up briefly with friends. He didn't stay in one place too long, however, because he was keeping closer track of who was there and who had yet to arrive than he normally did.

As soon as he felt sure that most of his guests, which included family, friends, and business associates, had arrived, he found Chelsea and pulled her away from her friends from college.

"You ready?"

She positively beamed at him. "Yes."

They'd spoken earlier and were in immediate and absolute agreement. Nothing seemed to have changed in the hours they'd had to think about it.

"Go get your brother, then," Seamus said.

Chelsea disappeared into the crowd. Seamus made his way to the bay window in the front of the house. From there, he could see the majority of this guests, and the rest could crowd into the front parlor when the time came.

Chelsea returned to his side with a very confused-looking Rhian in tow.

"What's up?" Rhian asked, looking over his shoulder nervously. He tried to shake loose Chelsea's hand but she held on fast.

"It seems I've been very foolish," Seamus said.

Rhian gave him his undivided attention, his hand tightening around his sister's. "Are you okay?"

Seamus clasped his arm warmly and smiled. "I'm fine. Mad at myself, really, but I intend to correct my error promptly."

"What are you talking about?" Rhian asked.

"I had an interesting chat with Garrick and Savannah earlier, and if it's all right with you, I'd like to take this opportunity to tell all these fine people, the people that mean the most to me and those who I have known best and for the longest, just what you mean to me."

Rhian looked at Chelsea, who smiled encouragingly, then back at Seamus. "Yeah. I mean, *yes.* I'd like that. But, are *you* sure?"

Rather than answer, Seamus picked up the glass and spoon he'd left on the table earlier and struck silver to crystal. Within seconds, he had the undivided attention of the entire room. As he'd suspected, the rest of his guests crowded from the adjoining rooms, too.

He gave it some time, mostly to allow all the attending members of the Morrison family to find their way to the front. Savannah and Garrick stood to one side, holding hands, with Savannah's parents at their backs. Several of her brothers were also there, along with their significant others. They all knew, of course, but Seamus though Rhian might like to have them close at a moment like this.

Everyone, family and acquaintances alike, were looking between Seamus, Chelsea, and Rhian in confusion. He'd not warned anyone except Chelsea of what he intended to do.

Seamus looked over at Rhian and found his grandson looked rather like a deer in headlights.

"Thank you all for coming," Seamus began, smiling at the crowd.

Silence fell.

"I'm not one for speeches at these things, but I'm hoping you'll forgive me for making an exception. There is someone very important to me, someone many of you know or have met, but who I have not been introducing properly. The reasons are long and unpleasant, but I will give you the shortest version possible."

Rhian turned to stare at Seamus. He looked stunned. And frightened. And hopeful.

The last bit meant that it would be a long time before Seamus stopped berating himself. Airing his family's unfortunate history seemed small in the face of that hope.

"Years ago, my daughter, Diane, left the area for some time. I recently learned that during that period, she gave birth to a baby boy." A murmur went through the crowd. Most of these people knew of Diane, and had likely noted her absence from Seamus's life over the past couple years. Now they'd know why. "She didn't tell anyone at the time, nor when she abandoned that boy a few years later before coming back to Boston. My very clever and frighteningly resourceful granddaughter, Chelsea, found out about this child and she tracked him down. She brought him to me, and I couldn't be prouder to call him my own."

All eyes were glued to Rhian now. Seamus thought many in the room were realizing how much he and Chelsea looked alike.

"So, I would very much like to introduce all of you to my grandson, Rhian Savage."

For a long moment, you could have heard a pin drop. Then the Morrisons began to clap, and everyone else immediately joined in.

Seamus turned to Rhian, who was a remarkable shade of pink, but looked happy. Really, really happy. "I'm sorry, Rhian, that I didn't do that a long time ago. I thought you didn't want it to be publicly known."

"I didn't. But then...I did," he admitted with a helpless shrug.

"I'm glad, then, that Savannah and Garrick set me straight. You and I will have to work on our communication, it seems, because I have never, ever, been ashamed of you, quite the opposite, and I would have gladly told everyone almost on day one, had I known you wouldn't mind."

"Well, yeah, that would have been too soon for me," Rhian conceded. "But I'm glad everyone knows now."

"Me, too."

"Me, three," Chelsea agreed. "Now my friends will stop thinking I'm secretly dating you, because that was really starting to gross me out."

Rhian shuddered. "Yeah, that will be good."

Chelsea hugged her brother and he hugged her back. Seamus couldn't love two people more. When she released him, Seamus gave into an urge he very rarely allowed himself to have.

He hugged Rhian, too.

Rhian clung to his grandfather and sternly lectured himself about how crying in front of all these people would be a terrible idea. It wasn't easy, though.

The crowd pressed closer, eager to speak with them, so Rhian eventually let go. He turned in time to be enveloped by the Morrison family.

He was always happy to see them, but tonight he was especially glad they were there. He used to find them all overwhelming, but now he relished every hug and pat on the back. He only got a little choked up again when Savannah's father offered to get up and claim him as his own, too.

Once he'd gotten through the family, Seamus wanted to introduce him to a few people, including distant relatives, which was a little weird. Rhian could tell there were plenty of other people who wanted an introduction, but Seamus was nice enough to limit it.

As soon as Rhian had moved on from the last of Seamus's introductions, an arm hooked around his neck.

"I didn't see that coming!" Jean-Michel said with a laugh.

Rhian grinned. "Well, now you know why I can invite riffraff like you to this here fancy party."

"Your grandfather is pretty cool," Henri agreed. "He invited me and Lisa and the kids to Christmas Eve dinner when he heard both our families can't visit this year."

"Did you accept?" Rhian asked eagerly. It would be great to have them there. And the Morrisons would go nuts to have more little kids around.

Henri hedged. "Well, I wasn't sure—"

"Seamus," Rhian said, touching his elbow to get his attention. "I mean, Grandfather," he amended.

Seamus turned immediately. "Yes, son?"

"Henri, Lisa, and the kids are coming for Christmas Eve."

"Wonderful. And you boys?" he asked.

Noel and Jean-Michel both looked stunned.

"I'm sorry, sir," Noel managed at last. "Jean-Michel and I are headed up to Quebec to see family during the break."

"Ah, well, perhaps Easter, then?"

"Uh, yes. Please. That would be nice."

Seamus turned back to another guest and Rhian grinned at the looks on all their faces.

"What can I say?" he said smugly. "I have a great family."

"Yeah, kid," Henri said, squeezing his shoulder. "You really do."

"Speaking of," Savannah said, appearing at Rhian's other shoulder. "If you boys would come with me, we're gathering in the den for a moment."

They all followed her, Rhian grinning at Savannah's brother—and Rhian's good friend—Lachlan hanging out in the doorway, monitoring who went in. The room was packed with only Morrisons, Seamus and Chelsea, and now his teammates.

Lachlan shut the door behind them.

Everyone was chatting, getting fresh drinks from the wet bar, and catching up, so Rhian hung back by the door to introduce Lachlan to his teammates. They took turns teasing him about his big night.

"Man, you're just *full* of surprises," Jean-Michel crowed. "What's next? Maybe you *are* a spy?"

Rhian chuckled. "Hardly. And I don't have any more secrets, I swear. You guys now know everything."

No sooner had the words left his lips that Savannah stood on one of the sturdier chairs in the room, Garrick's hand at her hip steadying her, and let out a sharp whistle.

Everyone turned to look at her. She smiled, winked at Rhian, and gestured for him to come join them.

It was time.

Before he went, Rhian threw his arm around Jean-Michel's neck and grinned at Noel and Henri.

"Okay, so maybe there is one more surprise.

About the Author

Samantha Wayland has three great loves in life; her family, writing books, and hockey. She is often found apologizing to the first for how much time and attention is taken up by the latter two, but they forgive her because they are awesome and she clearly doesn't deserve them.

Sam lives with her family—of both the two and four-legged variety—outside of Boston. She is a wicked passionate New Englander (born and raised) who has been known to wax rhapsodic about the Maine Coast, the mountains of New Hampshire and Vermont, and the sensible way in which her local brethren don't see a need for directional signals (blinkahs!). When she's not locked away in her home office, she can generally be found tucked in the corner of the local Thai place with other socially-starved authors and an adult beverage.

Her favorite things include mango martinis, tiny Chihuahuas with big attitude problems, and the Oxford comma.

Sam loves to hear from readers. Email her at samantha@samanthawayland.com or find her on Facebook (Samantha Wayland) or Twitter (@SamWayland).

Also by Samantha Wayland

With Grace

A man yearning to explore his sexual tastes but afraid to turn up the heat, the woman who loves him but is hungry for more spice...and the chef who craves them both.

When Grace, Philip and Mark find a mobster's flash drive full of incriminating information, they are quickly embroiled in a dangerous situation. They stay together for safety, but proximity ignites the sparks they've long been fighting to ignore.

When three friends dare to succumb to their appetites, they find the perfect recipe for love.

Destiny Calls

Patrick didn't think it would be a big deal to kiss Brandon, his best friend and fellow police officer. Hell, they'd done crazier things to escape a bar fight. But then he had no way of knowing just how hot it would be.

Destiny Matthews is not a woman who is afraid to ask for what she wants, and when she sees her two best friends kissing, she knows just what she's going to ask for. Before she can convince Patrick that he's not as straight as he likes to protest, Brandon is attacked by an unknown enemy.

While they fight to protect each other's lives, they prove time and again that they're even better at protecting their own hearts.

Fair Play

Hat Trick Book One

Savannah Morrison is the new athletic trainer for the Moncton Ice Cats, a professional hockey team in the wilds of New Brunswick. It's a good thing she's got plenty of knowledge and grit, because as the only woman trainer in the league, she has to work twice as hard to win the players' respect. The last thing on earth she would do is date one of them.

Twelve year hockey veteran Garrick LeBlanc isn't ready to hang up his skates, particularly since he hasn't figured out what the hell he's planning to do next. He needs the new trainer to keep him fit to play, and she's got the skills to do it. Too bad he lost his mind and hit on her the day they met. Now she hates his guts and he's made an art of ignoring her.

When the team is put up for sale, Garrick and Savannah have to work together to save their jobs and their team. Somewhere along the way, they discover Garrick isn't just a hockey player, Savannah isn't only passionate about her work, and just maybe they've got more in common than they thought.

Two Man Advantage

Hat Trick Book Two

Rhian is working his way up the ranks of professional hockey, with the dream of making it to the NHL getting closer every day. He's doing it alone—no family, no friends—and that's the way he likes it. Then he arrives in New Brunswick, and meets the Moncton Ice Cats. Suddenly, he's got friends—and even something that might be an honest-to-god crush.

Garrick is lonely and counting the days until his last season with the Ice Cats is over and he can move to Boston. When his girlfriend suggests he take a lover—as long that lover is a man and Garrick tells her all about it—he laughs it off. But damned if his buddy Rhian doesn't take on the starring role in his fantasies. Good thing Rhian is way too young—and straight—for what Garrick has in mind.

Rhian takes a chance when Garrick's increasingly confusing signals start making sense, and soon discovers he's bitten off more than he can chew. Sex with strangers is simple. Sex with his best friend? Complicated.

End Game

Hat Trick Book Three

Garrick LeBlanc never intended to fall in love with two people, but he has, and now he has to figure out what to do about it. He wants to make them happy, but is afraid he's doing just the opposite. To make matters worse, he's trapped in New Brunswick until the end of the hockey season, while his lovers are both in Boston.

Savannah Morrison has no one but herself to blame for practically shoving her lover into the arms of another man. After all, it was her idea that Garrick take a lover while they are separated for the season. She loves Garrick with all her heart, but how the hell is she going to share him with Rhian?

Rhian Savage used to have such a simple life. Now he's in love, his dreams of skating on an NHL team are coming true, and he keeps spotting a strangely familiar face in the crowds. To top it all off, he has to see Savannah every day. He knows she's Garrick's real future, but he doesn't have the balls to do the right thing for all of them and end it—until his life goes sideways. As usual.

Now Rhian is alone, Garrick is heartbroken, and Savannah—the one person Rhian figured would celebrate his departure—is beating down his door. What the hell is up with that?

Crashing the Net

Mike comes to Moncton wanting nothing more than to play for the Ice Cats and finally live on his own terms. He's broke, bruised, and covered from head to toe in cheap lube, but he isn't going to let that stop him. All he needs is a place to live and some time to figure out how to reconcile who he really is with who everyone wants him to be.

Dumping three gallons of lube on the new kid is just another day at the office for Alexei. He knows exactly who he is: a goalie on the ice, a prankster in the locker room, and a man who knows better than to share his private life with anyone. He's let people in before and it's taught him that if he can't have what he really wants, it's better to be alone.

Despite their apparent differences, an unlikely friendship grows. Neither of them could ever have guessed how much they really have in common.

Home & Away

You can build a team, but you have to find your home.

Rupert Smythe is fond of many things. Callum Morrison isn't one of them.

Rupert is a quiet, thoughtful business man and, sadly, a total wimp. Maybe not the ideal candidate to run a professional hockey team, but he signed on to do it anyway. As his life has reminded him on an almost daily basis since, this isn't the most brilliant idea he's ever had. And that was before Callum showed up.

Being in the spotlight is just part of being a professional athlete, but Callum needs a break. He arrives in Moncton unannounced, determined to help grow the team he just bought, and under the assumption he'd be welcome. Possibly he should have tried to make a better first impression.

Callum figures he can push through the rest of the summer, never expecting two kids, a host of friends, and his growing feelings for Rupert to derail everything he has ever believed about what he wanted, and what he could have.

Out Of Her League

Lachlan Morrison's family likes to tell people that he's shy, but that's like saying the sky is sort of blue, or good hockey is just a little bit rough. Lachlan knows perfectly well he's a social disaster and works hard to humiliate himself as infrequently as possible.

Then Michaela Price, the most beautiful woman he's ever laid eyes on, moves to town, and she needs a friend.

Michaela knows she's no prize. As a nationally-known disgrace, she's pretty used to being stared at and having to chase photographers off the neighbors' roofs. She wouldn't wish her life on anyone, and certainly has no intention of inflicting herself on poor Lachlan Morrison, who literally cannot speak in her presence.

But then, going back to school isn't what she expected. It turns out her new life is just as lonely as the old version, and she only knows one person in town.

Checking It Twice

After four years with Alexei, there are a few things Mike knows with absolute certainty: he loves Alexei, Alexei loves him, and Alexei gives the very best gifts. This Christmas is no exception, though Mike is having a hell of a time figuring out what, exactly, Alexei's gift *is*.

Alexei knows his gift this year is going to blow Mike's mind, but in the meantime, it's pretty hilarious watching Mike try to figure out what it is. Granted, Alexei does have a lot of surprises in store for Mike this week, and it sure as hell isn't frankincense and myrrh.